RIDERS ON THE WIND

John Hauck and his wife are hired by the proprietor of the Wild West show in which they used to perform to track down his kidnapped daughter. Their search takes them across the country, following a twisted trail of lies and deception, fighting all the way against the sinister Dement and his gang. Sioux chief Otoktay joins his old friend Hauck on the way, but how will these old-timers deal with a changing world as they reprise former battles?

VANCE TILLMAN

RIDERS ON THE WIND

Complete and Unabridged

LINFORD
Leicester

First published in Great Britain in 2011 by
Robert Hale Limited
London

First Linford Edition
published 2013
by arrangement with
Robert Hale Limited
London

A catalogue record for this book is available
from the British Library.

ISBN 978–1–4448–1673–0

Published by
F. A. Thorpe (Publishing)
Anstey, Leicestershire

Set by Words & Graphics Ltd.
Anstey, Leicestershire
Printed and bound in Great Britain by
T. J. International Ltd., Padstow, Cornwall

This book is printed on acid-free paper

1

It was a bright morning; roosters were calling, dogs barking and cattle bells ringing in the pastures. The two riders had risen early and had already passed the farmhouse just as lights were appearing in the kitchen windows. They were a man and a woman, no longer young but fit and well-honed. The man was lean yet strongly built; the woman small and light-framed. She wore a conventional riding outfit that could not hide the graceful bearing of her Nez Percé origin.

'Looks like somebody's havin' a spot of trouble up ahead,' the man said.

The woman nodded. Her keen eyes had seen the wagon too, stranded by the side of the road. As they got closer they could see that the left fore-wheel had come off. A man was standing near by; he had unhitched the horses and fastened them to a tree.

'By the look of the way the front of the buggy has dropped, I'd say there was a good chance the axle-box must've come loose,' the man said.

A few moments later his surmise was proved correct when the woman spotted the missing item lying in the dust by the side of the road. They halted long enough for her to retrieve it, then they rode on till they came alongside the wagon.

'This what you're lookin' for?' the man said.

The man with the wagon looked up, shielding his eyes from the sun. 'Say, where'd you find that? I bin searchin' for a good hour an' couldn't see no trace.'

'You've got the lady to thank for that. Don't much escape her notice.' The two riders dismounted.

'My name is Hauck, John Hauck, and this is Julia.'

The man held out his hand. 'Riley,' he replied, 'Wendell Riley. Sure am pleased to meet you.'

'Let's get that axle fixed,' Hauck said.

The two men set to work. While they did so the Indian woman looked admiringly at the polished buckles and red rosettes on the horses' harnesses. The horses themselves had been carefully brushed and combed and the man looked equally well-groomed in a black suit and boots and with his hair slicked back. He was dusty and hot now but he had obviously made a big effort to look smart. It didn't take long to get the buggy fixed.

'Nice rig,' Hauck commented as he stood back. 'Goin' some place special?'

'County fair. Got to pick up my gal on the way. She'll have been expectin' me. Sure hope she ain't gone with anyone else.'

'Better get movin',' Hauck said.

The man hesitated. He was young and suddenly seemed embarrassed. 'Sure appreciate you folks helpin' me,' he said. 'Say, why don't you come along? It ain't but a few miles to town.'

Hauck turned towards the woman. He couldn't mistake the gleam in her eye. 'Sure,' he said.

'Why don't I see you there? I could introduce you to some of the folks.'

For the first time the woman spoke. 'That would be real nice,' she said. She smiled and glanced towards the buggy. 'Like he says, better get movin'. You don't want to keep your lady waitin' longer than she has already.'

Riley grinned; it made him look little more than a boy. Climbing into the buggy he started his team on a quick trot down the road, leaning back to wave at them as he went.

'Something about him reminds me of you,' Julia said to her partner. 'When I first met you. Remember?'

'That was a long time ago,' he replied.

'Don't seem like it though.'

The man smiled and reaching into his pocket pulled out a small package.

'You still carry that thing around with you?'

'Sure do,' he replied.

It was a parfleche made from tanned buffalo hide, painted with geometric designs which had once been bright but were now faded with usage. Inside was a string of beads made from animal claws.

'Good medicine,' she said.

'The best,' he replied.

He replaced the parfleche in the pocket of his jacket. 'Come on, Ealaothek-kaunis,' he said. It was her Nez Percé name and it meant Birds Landing. 'Guess we're goin' to the county fair.'

As they got closer to town the roads became thick with wagons, buckboards and top-buggies, most of them gaily decorated, making their way towards the town which soon came in sight — a cluster of frame buildings and stores around a central square with some shade trees. A newly painted sign read *Scott Corner*. People had congregated in the town square, their conveyances lining the adjacent streets. It was an animated scene. Around three sides of the square booths had been set up and on the fourth side there were trestle tables loaded with foodstuffs. At one were platters laden with baked hams, fried chickens and other cooked meats; at another there were pumpkins, watermelons and apples and on one more jams, cakes, cookies and pies. An elderly lady in a blue gingham dress was serving lemonade. Further off, on the edge of town, some corrals were filled with livestock. There were farm implements and, in pride of place, a mechanical threshing machine. In the streets people were thronging round a series of stalls and from somewhere a piano tinkled. Hauck and Birds Landing dismounted and tied their horses to a hitchrack outside a drugstore on the fringes of the most populated area and made their way inside. There was a soda fountain and people sat together on little revolving stools. It was quite busy but they were soon served. They were just about to get up and leave when

Wendell Riley came bursting through the door, accompanied by a fair-haired girl wearing a white muslin dress.

'Figured I'd run into you,' he said. 'What'd I say, Hester? Didn't I say they must be somewhere around?'

Without pausing for breath he came up to Hauck and Birds Landing. 'Thanks to you I just made it in time,' he said. He turned to the girl. 'Hester, I'd like for you to meet Mr Hauck and Julia.'

The girl smiled and held out her hand without any suggestion of awkwardness.

'Have you seen around?' Wendell asked.

'Just about to do it,' Birds Landing replied.

'Come on, we'll show you.'

They were on their way outside when their path to the doorway was blocked by three men. They were mean-looking and they all wore sidearms.

'Excuse me,' the boy began.

The men stood immobile. Some of

the customers in the drugstore made for an exit at the rear. Others watched with close attention.

'Excuse me,' Wendell repeated.

One of the men moved a fraction to one side. 'Go on out, boy,' he said. 'We ain't got no quarrel with you or your girl.'

Riley looked bemused. Hauck stepped forward.

'It's OK, Wendell. Do as he says. Take Hester outside. We'll meet up with you later.'

The boy looked unsure. Hester pushed at him from behind and after another moment's hesitation he moved to the door. With a last glance back he led his girl into the street.

For the first time Hauck confronted the three men. His blue eyes were hard and the man who had spoken looked away for a moment before turning to his henchmen. Hauck remained silent.

'This is a nice town,' the man said. 'We don't hold truck with no Injun lovers.'

' 'Specially not a squaw-man,' one of the others added.

'Ain't that right?' the third one said, turning his head to address the remaining customers. Most of them looked uncomfortable. One of them, a fat man wearing a black suit and string tie, responded with a feeble: 'Sure.'

'What's more,' the leader of the group said, 'we aim to teach you a lesson. Just to make sure that you understand the situation.'

'Pistol-whip 'em,' someone shouted from the back of the room.

The man took one step forward. Before he had time to take a second Hauck's fist had crashed into his face, shattering his nose and sending him reeling backwards.

'Why you — ' he began.

His hand moved towards the gun which was placed butt forwards in its holster, but even as he drew it something glistened through the air and buried itself in his throat. Birds Landing had thrown her knife with deadly accuracy. The man hit the floor and lay there gurgling as blood spouted from his mouth. The other two men had drawn their guns but Hauck was quicker. The gun in his hand spat lead and they both went down, one of them firing his pistol harmlessly into the ceiling as he fell. After the noise and unexpected violence there was an eerie calm. Hauck turned round.

'You!' he said.

A man at the back of the room wearing fancy duds looked up in alarm.

'Who, me? I ain't done nothin.' It was the man who had advocated the pistol-whipping.

'You can apologize on their behalf to me and the lady,' Hauck said. 'After that you can get out of town and if I ever see you again I'll kill you.'

The man looked about him as if to elicit some support but if that was his aim none was forthcoming.

'I . . . I'm sorry,' he said. 'Real sorry.'

'OK, apology accepted. Now git and remember what I said.'

Quickly the man slinked through the back door. Hauck turned to the man behind the counter.

'Sorry about this,' he said, 'but all you folks saw that this was none of our doing.' He reached into his pocket, drew out some dollar bills and threw them on the counter.

'That should cover any damage. Now I guess somebody had better roust out the marshal. And the undertaker.'

Hauck and Birds Landing turned on their heels and walked out of the door. Outside everything was as normal, with the people enjoying the holiday spirit.

'What now?' Birds Landing said.

'I think Wendell Riley and his girl are waitin' for us someplace,' Hauck replied.

Birds Landing was for leaving town but Hauck was obstinate. They would leave when they were ready. Word quickly got around and Hauck was conscious of the fact that some people were watching out for them. Nobody seemed prepared to regard them too openly. People were aware of how quickly and ruthlessly they had responded when they were threatened. However, Hauck got the impression that they were not regarded without a certain favour. It was only later in the day that the marshal caught up with him and the reason became clearer.

'I gather you had some trouble in the drugstore,' he began.

Hauck was quick to arrive at a judgement of people and the marshal gave a good impression. He was a thin, dry individual with greying hair and a face lined with wrinkles, although he was probably not older than forty. The lines spread from his eyes and there were two deep indentations either side of his nose to the corners of his mouth.

'Nothin' we couldn't handle,' Hauck replied.

'So I gather.'

'Talk to any of the folks that was there,' Hauck said. 'They'll tell you how it was.'

'I know how it was,' the marshal replied.

They were walking round the display of farm implements.

'The name's Harper,' the marshal said. 'Ben Harper.'

Hauck introduced himself and Birds Landing.

'To tell you the truth,' the marshal said, 'you've kinda done me a favour. I've been havin' some trouble from those varmints for a whiles. I guess it was just a question of time.'

Dusk was drawing down and in the town square lights were being rigged up in the trees.

'Dancin' tonight,' the marshal said. 'Why don't you stick around?'

Hauck looked at Birds Landing. 'Sure,' he said.

Just then Wendell Riley came by. 'Mr Hauck,' he said. 'I heard what happened at the drugstore.' He looked hesitantly at the marshal. 'Man, that was some show you put on!'

Hauck shook his head. 'Had no

choice,' he replied.

'If you folks need a place to stay after the dance,' the marshal said, 'I could recommend the Regent.'

Riley looked eagerly from one to another of the four of them. 'Hey, no need to do that,' he said. 'You could stay right out at the farm. I know Ma and Pa would be only too happy.'

'That's OK,' Hauck replied. 'Birds Landing and me, we're used to sleepin' under the stars.'

'Well, the offer stands,' Riley replied. 'Just think about it. We've got plenty of room.'

'I'll need you folks just to clear up a few formalities,' the marshal said. 'Whatever your plans are, how about you check in with me tomorrow mornin'?'

'No problem,' Hauck replied. 'We'll be there.'

Lanterns had been hung in the branches of the trees. A couple of fiddlers began to tune up and they were joined by an accordion. Some of the older women began to clap and keep time with their feet. A few couples commenced to dance under the trees.

'If you'll excuse us?' Wendell said, taking Hester by the arm and leading her to the open space which now served as a dance floor.

'A nice pair,' the marshal said.

The musicians began to play a waltz and Hauck looked at Birds Landing.

'What are we waitin' for?' she said.

The marshal watched as Hauck put his arms about her waist. They moved well, better than most of the younger participants. The marshal watched them for a while before turning away and walking off down the street. *Odd*, he was thinking. *They don't seem to have been affected in any way by what happened earlier.* Most people would have been put off their stride. Not them. He looked back. There were a lot of people dancing now and he didn't see them for a moment until they came swirling back into view. The waltz had finished and the musicians had struck

15

up a long gliding tune which he recognized as an old Bohemian melody. There were quite a lot of Bohemians and Swedes and some Czechs in the area. They all got on well. He felt a sudden sense of shame that the Indian lady had been treated the way she had. The way she had dealt with it, nobody was likely to try it again.

It was late. The land was drenched in moonlight and in the fields the straw stacks cast deep shadows. Most of the townsfolk had retired for the night and along the dusty roads the last of the farm dwellers were making their way homewards. Hauck and Birds Landing were riding behind Riley's top-buggy. In the end they had been persuaded to go back with him to the farm. He had dropped Hester off at the farmstead where she lived with her parents and two brothers. Presently the road took a dip, then, as it climbed again to top the brow of a low hill Riley's farm came into view, etched against the deep azure-blue of the sky. The farmhouse was dark apart from one light in a side window. Behind it there were the shadowy outlines of a barn and between the two was a windmill. Before they had even reached the gate Hauck rode up alongside the wagon and signalled to Riley to halt.

'Just about home,' Riley began.

Hauck held a finger to his lips.

'What is it?' Riley said.

'I don't know. Somethin's not right.'

'What do you mean?'

'The only sound I can hear is the creak of that windmill,' Hauck said. 'I can smell pigs. I ain't no farmer, but shouldn't they be making some sort of sound? What about dogs? You got a dog?'

Riley listened closely. 'You're right,' he said. 'Ol' Brownie shoulda been barkin' by now.'

'Wait here,' Hauck said. 'I'll take a look.'

'I'm comin' with you.'

'Don't make any noise.'

Leaving the horses and the buggy in

17

the charge of Birds Landing, Hauck and Riley opened the gate and moved silently up the path to the farmhouse. As they approached Hauck saw something lying in the yard. They moved quickly forward. It was the dog. He had been shot. Before Hauck could stop him Riley had rushed to the door. It swung open at his push. Hauck pulled his gun out of its holster and followed him inside the house. It was dark, the only light seeping out from the partly open door of the kitchen. Without pausing Riley rushed forward followed by Hauck. He pushed at the kitchen door but it was jammed. He pushed harder. Hauck tugged at his sleeve but he was frantic now. Rushing at the door, he put his shoulder to it and it opened far enough for them to see a woman's legs. She was jammed behind the door but there was sufficient room to step through. Riley let out an unearthly howl and fell to his knees.

The kitchen was a scene of slaughter. Blood had gathered in a pool on the floor and the walls were spattered with it. The bodies of Riley's parents lay twisted in death. They had both been shot a number of times. Hauck took in the scene at once and, leaving Riley where he kneeled, moved quickly back to the parlour.

He looked round. Nothing seemed to have been disturbed. He saw a stairwell and started up the stairs. Three rooms led off from the landing. He looked in each but there was nothing untoward. He knew that he would find no one in the house but he checked anyway. Whoever had done this was clear away by now. Below him he could hear Riley sobbing and moaning.

He came back down the stairs, ran out into the yard and went round the house towards the barn at the back. The hog corral was alongside; the pigs had been slaughtered too. He turned back and entered the barn. It was very dark inside but he could see that there were stalls for horses. They were empty. He guessed that the killers had taken the horses with them.

He looked about and it didn't take him long to discover a piece of cloth attached to a wooden post by one of the stalls. Somebody had caught his sleeve while getting the horses out. He slipped it into his pocket, then made his way out of the barn. As he moved to the rear of the farm he could see plenty of sign indicating the passage of riders. He hadn't noticed anything unusual in the way of tracks when they were coming along the road. It seemed like whoever had done this had ridden across country. He reckoned the tracks were already quite old. The attack on the farm had taken place in broad daylight while most of the people living near by were at the county fair.

He made his way back to the house but did not go inside. Instead he made his way down the path to where Birds Landing was waiting with the horses and the buggy. Quickly he explained the situation to her. She already had a pretty good intuitive understanding of what had happened.

'Give Riley some time and then I'll go and get him. He can't stay here. We'll take him back to Hester's farm.'

They sat together in the buggy. The night was still and the sky seemed huge above the flat land. Presently they saw a figure emerge from the house, silhouetted against the light thrown from the lamp in the kitchen. Riley came down the path and stood by the side of the buggy, looking back at the house. He seemed to have recovered a measure of composure. Birds Landing went up to him and put her arm around his shoulder before helping him into the carriage. Hauck had tied their horses to the back of the buggy. He flicked the reins. The team responded and he manoeuvred the buggy so it was pointing back the way they had come. Nobody spoke till they reached Hester's farm, then Birds Landing said to Hauck:

'Why don't you leave things here to me while you get back to town and roust out the marshal? Join me here later.'

Hauck nodded. 'Guess the quicker the marshal gets on to this the better,' he said.

'I'll see to the buggy and the horses as well,' she added.

Hauck untied his own horse, stepped into the leather and set off down the road to town. He looked back once to see Birds Landing helping Riley up the path to the farmhouse. Light spilled on to the porch as the front door was opened.

The marshal's office was closed and Hauck had to ask a passer-by the way to his house. He lived in a small frame building on the edge of town and Hauck was relieved to see the lights were still on despite the lateness of the hour. He tied his horse to a hitchrack in the yard and knocked on the door. It was soon opened by a tall lady whom Hauck took to be the marshal's wife. Quickly but without going into the gory details he outlined his purpose in calling so late. Before he had finished the marshal himself appeared in the doorway.

'It's Mr Hauck, isn't it?' he said. 'It's OK, Barbara. Come on in.'

Hauck found himself in a cosy and tastefully decorated room. Barbara, realizing something serious was afoot, made her way to the kitchen to brew some coffee while Hauck explained what had happened at the farm. When he had finished the marshal looked grim.

'I can't believe it,' he said at last. 'They were such decent folks. We've not had anything like this happen in years.'

'It should be easy to follow the killers,' Hauck said. 'They've left a trail a mile wide.'

'Who would do somethin' like that?' The marshal seemed bemused.

'I got a hunch,' Hauck said.

The marshal looked at him.

'Those three *hombres* this afternoon,' Hauck continued. 'Maybe there were others. Plenty people saw what happened. They might have known where Riley lived. They might have decided to exact a little revenge.'

Barbara appeared with the coffee. She seemed even more upset than the marshal.

'Poor Wendell,' she said. 'I've knowed his folks since I can't remember when.'

She poured black coffee into china cups. The marshal had been ruminating on Hauck's words as he sipped the coffee.

'You could be right,' he said. 'At least we ain't got anythin' else to work on. Now you mention it, there have been some mean-lookin' *hombres* hangin' about town just recently. I never gave it too much mind. Figured they was just a bunch o' hardcases passin' through. Apart from this afternoon, though, there ain't been any real trouble. The county fair passed off just fine.'

'If I'm right,' Hauck said, 'they've got to be round these parts for a reason. They was headin' west. What's the next town?'

'That'd be Prairie Junction,' the marshal said. 'It's a good ride.'

'Prairie Junction?'

'The spur line just reached that far,' the marshal said. 'They're aimin' to build the railroad out this way next.'

'Thought they'd have done it by now,' Hauck said. 'Seems to be pretty well settled.'

'That's just it. I reckon they think we're well catered for one way and another. More money to be made extendin' into the West.'

Hauck was thinking hard. 'I got a personal stake in this,' he said. 'If it's OK with you, Marshal, I think me and Julia will head for Prairie Junction. I'm pretty sure that's where the trail will lead us anyway. If you can get up a posse first thing in the mornin' then come on behind.'

'What, you aimin' to go right now?' the marshal said.

'No time like the present.' Hauck turned to Barbara. 'Thanks for the coffee, ma'am.'

'It's nothin',' she replied. 'Won't you stay for a bite to eat?'

'That's a real nice offer, but I'd best be on my way.' He turned to the marshal. 'Me an' Julia may be old-timers but we know how to follow a trail. We'll catch up with 'em even if you don't.'

'I'll wire ahead,' the marshal said.

Hauck looked slightly nonplussed. 'Whatever it takes,' he said. He went out through the door and mounted his horse. 'So long,' he said.

The marshal and his wife watched him gallop away. 'You know,' the marshal commented. 'he might be an old-timer — and his woman too, but somehow I'd back them against any gang of outlaws you care to name.'

When Hauck had taken the decision to ride off straight away, it was not entirely because he wanted to hit the trail early; it was because he didn't want to involve the marshal or Barbara in anything untoward. Now, as he swung back down the road towards the Hester ranch, he was on the alert and his hand hovered over the Winchester .22-calibre pump-action repeater in its scabbard. When he was clear of town and about a third of the way back to the Hester farm he swung off the trail into a draw made shadowy by trees, listening carefully.

At first he could hear nothing but the sighing of the wind in the branches, then he became aware of another sound: the muffled drumming of horses' hoofs. He listened attentively. There were two riders and they were coming from the direction of the farm. Suddenly the shadow of a smile crossed his face. He recognized the sound of one of the horses; it was Birds Landing's brown-and-white paint. It took him only a moment's thought to work out that the other probably belonged to Riley and that he had persuaded Birds Landing to accompany him to town. He didn't want to alarm them, so he touched his spurs to his horse's flanks.

At the same moment, as his horse stepped forward, there was a spurt of flame from above him and the crashing roar of a rifle shot which tore into the trunk of a nearby tree. In an instant he had sprung from the saddle and as another shot reverberated in the night he fired at the stab of flame with his long-barrelled Colt Cavalry revolver. There was a scream of anguish, then a body came hurtling out of a tree which overlooked the trail from town, landing on the earth with a loud thud. Hauck moved forward to where he had a better view of the body. It was clear that the man was dead.

Hauck moved quickly back to his horse, swung himself into the saddle and, regaining the trail, rode to meet the approaching riders, who seemed to have temporarily halted in the aftermath of the shooting. He knew that Birds Landing would have recognized his own appaloosa and, sure enough, they were waiting for his arrival. When he had come alongside he explained what had happened.

'The varmint must have been waitin' for me comin' back along the trail,' he said. 'But what are you doin' here?'

'Mr Riley didn't want to wait around. He wants to find whoever was responsible for . . . ' Birds Landing hesitated.

'It's OK,' Riley said. He turned to Hauck. 'Like Julia says, I don't want to waste any time. I want to find whoever killed my parents.'

Hauck nodded. 'I can understand that,' he said.

'I just can't face the prospect of sittin' about doin' nothin',' Riley added.

'I said I'd come with him to meet you,' Birds Landing said.

There was complete understanding between Birds Landing and Hauck. Again Hauck nodded. He turned to Riley.

'What about Hester?' he said. 'She's maybe needin' some support right now.'

'I wouldn't be any good,' Riley said. 'Not feelin' the way I do. Besides, she has her ma and pa.'

There was silence for a moment in the wake of his words.

'OK,' Hauck said at last. 'There'll be some hard ridin' and things could get real tough. Me an' Julia, we can look after ourselves. But what about you? D'you reckon you'd be up to it?'

Riley's face looked taut in the moonlight. 'Try me,' he said.

Hauck smiled briefly. 'Yeah,' he commented. He looked from Riley to Birds Landing.

'What are we waitin' for?' he said. 'Let's ride.'

2

They rode for a couple of hours before Hauck called a halt for the night. Riley was for carrying on but Hauck realized that they would be all the better in the morning for some rest. In fact it wouldn't be too long until dawn broke. It had been a long and very hard day and night and it seemed an age since they had first helped Riley with his broken buggy. Birds Landing had been far-sighted enough to pack her saddle-bags with provisions. Hauck reckoned they could stock up and acquire a saddle-horse somewhere along the line, probably at Prairie Junction. As soon as they had built a camp Riley succumbed to the strains and exertions of the past few hours and, despite himself, fell asleep. Hauck sat with Birds Landing.

'We need to take extra care,' he said. 'You're thinkin' of that bushwhacker who lay in ambush for you?'

'Yeah. They might just try somethin' again.'

After a time Hauck shook out a bedroll and climbed in. Birds Landing was about to join him when she glanced at the sleeping form of Riley.

'He's a big boy,' Hauck said. 'Besides, we're married.'

'Some people wouldn't think so.'

'The hell with what people think,' Hauck said. 'Since when have we worried about that?'

Birds Landing smiled, then slipped in beside him. For a while neither of them spoke, then Birds Landing turned her face to Hauck's.

'Feels good, doesn't it?' she said.

'Always does,' Hauck said.

She snuggled closer to him. 'Not that. You know what I mean. Bein' here, under the stars, headin' back West.'

Hauck looked down at her eager face. 'Sure thing,' he said. 'We bin gone too long.'

Two days' riding brought them to

Prairie Junction. It was well-named. Not only was it on the railroad but it lay on a divide between the farming country to the east and the open grasslands to the west. Already Hauck and Birds Landing were breathing more freely. They could feel the pull of the wilderness stretching away ahead of them. As if in acknowledgement of it, Birds Landing had changed her riding outfit for something more serviceable. There was plenty of sign indicating that the men they were pursuing had passed that way. Birds Landing gave her opinion that there were eight of them and that, in addition to their own mounts, they had a couple of pack-horses.

'If we're right,' Hauck said, 'that makes a dozen of 'em all told, including the three in the drugstore and the one who was waitin' to bushwhack me.'

'Which means you've already dealt with a quarter of them,' Riley commented.

Hauck grinned. 'Guess that's right,'

he said. 'Never was no good at arithmetic.'

Hauck didn't expect to find the gunslicks at Prairie Junction and he was right. They made enquiries but nobody had seen anything of them.

'They had a start of us,' he remarked, 'but not a big one. Not more than twelve hours. I'd have maybe expected to catch 'em up along the way but they seem to be drivin' on hell for leather.'

Leaving their horses at the livery stable, the three of them made their way to the railroad track. There was little to be seen apart from the tank house, a tall windmill with its sails turning in the breeze, and a diminishing line of telegraph poles. A train was waiting on the tracks but there seemed to be little activity until, after a time, a man with a hammer appeared from a hut on the opposite side of the tracks and began hammering at something beneath the train. They made their way to where he was working.

'Howdy,' Hauck said.

The man was bending over and now seemed to see them for the first time. Extricating himself from under the chassis, he straightened up.

'Howdy.' He wiped a hand across his brow. 'Bet you cain't guess what these wheels are made of?' he said.

Hauck shook his head.

'Paper,' the man said and, seeing the puzzled expression on Birds Landing's face, went on, 'that's right. Paper. Leastways that's what I heard. Maybe these is different. Someone told me that, properly prepared, paper is one of the toughest substances there is. Wheels are subjected to enormous amounts of hydraulic pressure. Wood cracks, steel becomes brittle. I guess paper's not only strong but elastic too.'

He paused, regarding them closely.

'Afraid you've got a wait if it's the train you're wantin',' he said. 'Ain't due to leave till day after tomorrow.'

'Where's she headed?'

'She'll take you as far as Council Bluffs. That's the terminus for the

Chicago and North Western Railway. The Union Pacific will take you clear to San Francisco.' He seemed to take a pride in giving out these details and with only a brief pause he began to muse reflectively.

'Took me a ride one time. From Chicago. In a Pullman car. Ever been in one of those things? Spring mattress, linen sheets. And the food! Fresh fish caught at the last station along the way. Beefsteak, broiled chicken, hot rolls and cornbread. The places! Dixon, Clinton, Cedar Rapids, Woodbine, Council Bluffs, Omaha.'

He reeled off the towns along the route with obvious relish before pulling himself up almost with a start.

'But you folks probably got somethin' better to do than hear me ramblin' on.'

'It's interestin',' Hauck said.

'Come back day after tomorrow. That is, if you're plannin' to take a ride.'

They walked away but not in the direction of town. Instead Hauck started along the parallel lines of smooth shining rail which stretched straight across the featureless prairie, where only a few grazing cattle disturbed the empty silence of the morning. Riley was restless. Disappointed at not having encountered the outlaws in Prairie Junction, he was anxious to get back on the trail. Hauck seemed to have other ideas. After walking for some distance he suddenly stopped as if he had come to a conclusion.

'I think we might just take a ticket to ride,' he said.

The next day Hauck and Birds Landing headed out of town, following the line of the tracks. The country was flat and desolate, with patches of ploughed earth and occasional clumps of trees. After about a dozen miles of riding they saw in the distance a low line of bluffs with a feathery fringe of cottonwoods and willows and when they got closer they saw that the railroad track ran across a narrow stream on a small trestle-bridge.

'You figure those owlhoots might be aimin' to ambush the train?' Birds Landing said.

'Yeah. And I reckon this is as good a spot as any.'

'I figured that too. But we ain't seen no sign.'

Hauck raised himself in the saddle. As far as he could see the only movements were the shadows of clouds scudding across the prairie. 'Maybe I got this all wrong,' he said. Neither of them believed it.

The following day presented something of a contrasting scene at the railhead. Things seemed positively bustling. In particular there was a small party of emigrants bound eventually for Cheyenne and Sioux City. Hauck, Birds Landing and Riley took their places in one of the carriages. The migrants and a few other passengers had occupied the three other carriages, so they had the compartment pretty much to themselves. As they waited for the train to start a buckboard pulled up and leaning out of the carriage window, Hauck could see some boxes being loaded. Turning back to his companions, he said:

'I think we made the right decision to catch the train.' Birds Landing merely nodded but Riley looked bemused.

'Listen,' Hauck said. 'I got a hunch that this train is carryin' somethin' valuable in those boxes, I don't know what — money, bullion. I suspected somethin' of the sort. Those outlaw varmints didn't head this way without a reason. They've gone on beyond the town. I figure it's a good bet they'll be waitin' somewhere down the line.'

'What! You think they're plannin' to rob the train?'

'I reckon there's a good chance. If they do, we'll be ready for 'em. If I'm wrong, we ain't lost much. We can get back on their trail easy enough.'

'If you're wrong they could be anywhere,' Riley said.

Hauck glanced at Birds Landing. 'Believe me, she can follow a trail better than a bloodhound. She's a Nez Percé. And when it comes to it, I ain't so very far behind.'

Time passed and the train remained stationary. The buckboard moved away and after a time the door to their carriage opened and two more passengers got in. One was a man in his twenties with a stubbled face, the other was an older man, wearing a frock-coat which seemed too big for him and a stovepipe hat which sat uncomfortably atop his head. The old man acknowledged Hauck and his companions with a brief nod and sat in a seat opposite. The other man moved towards the front of the carriage. Riley watched them unconcernedly, then turned back to Hauck.

'If you don't mind me askin',' he said, 'but how long have you two been together?'

'Thirty-five years,' Hauck replied.

'That's a real long time. You must have seen some changes?'

'Sure have. Things is altogether different now.'

'What made you come out this way?'

Hauck didn't mind the young man's questions. 'Ever hear of Kemble Rheinhardt?' he asked.

Riley looked blank.

'Rheinhardt's Travellin' Wild West Show?' Hauck prompted.

'Don't mean nothin' to me.'

'Well, Rheinhardt is the proprietor of a kinda circus show that acts out scenes from what folks back East like to call the Wild West. To cut a long story short, me an' Birds Landing — Julia that is — got ourselves employed. We put on a little feature about mountain men and the openin' up of the Rocky Mountains. Don't get me wrong. It was a good livin' and we weren't complainin'. The few occasions we met Rheinhardt he treated us real well. But I could see that Birds Landing wasn't too happy and I was beginnin' to feel that way myself.'

He paused and Birds Landing took

41

up the story. 'We was in some place near Buffalo. We done our act and then we just walked out on it all,' she concluded.

'It's hard to put into words,' Hauck said, 'but since we left I've done some thinkin' and I reckon I've figured it out. You see, we was doin' things in that act which we done for real when we were young. It kinda took the starch out of it. It almost seemed like we was betrayin' ourselves in some way. Guess I ain't makin' much sense.'

Riley shook his head. 'No,' he said. 'I think I see what you mean. Kinda like a burlesque.'

'It was underminin' what we'd done in our past. Anyways, we decided we'd had enough and so we started back west.'

'And that's when you met me,' Riley said. 'Gee, I sure seem to have messed up your plans.'

'We're still headin' west,' Hauck said. 'Guess we're just takin' a detour.'

Further conversation was interrupted

by the blowing of a whistle and, with what sounded like a small explosion under the wheels, the train began to roll forward. Dense clouds of smoke billowed past the window. There was a sudden jolt and the train came to a temporary halt before beginning to move again, building up speed to a steady twenty miles an hour. Hauck glanced at the others.

'OK,' he said. 'Should take us about three-quarters of an hour to reach the bridge over the creek. You know what to do if the train is attacked.'

The others nodded. Riley's face was grim; Hauck could tell how nervous he had become and for a fleeting moment wondered whether he had done the right thing to bring him along. Maybe he should have left him at Prairie Junction. Maybe they should have ridden to the creek and not boarded the train at all. It was too late now to do anything about it.

The train was moving smoothly, creeping like an ant steadily across the dreary landscape. Hauck watched through the window, looking for any sign of activity; eventually he stood up and without a word to the others moved through the intervening carriages to the front of the train. Soon after that Birds Landing rose and made her way to the platform at the back. The train rattled on. Suddenly there was another lurch and the carriages seemed to slow. Looking forward, Hauck saw that the engine was moving away from the railcars. It was a strange sensation and at first he didn't know what had happened. The carriages seemed to be gliding along while the gap between them and the engine widened. The thick black smoke which had been streaming from the smokestack grew thinner. The railcars were slowing perceptibly now and Hauck realized what had happened. Someone had detached the cars from the engine! At the same moment a hubbub of sound assailed his ears. There were shouts from the carriage in which most of the migrants were situated. The train whistle blew and then, from somewhere off to the side, there came the sound of galloping horses. Looking ahead, Hauck could see willow trees and cottonwoods. They had reached the creek; the engine had already crossed by the wooden bridge and was coming to a halt on the other side.

Having been temporarily disorientated, Hauck was fully aware now of what was happening. A shot rang out, clanging against metal, and then another thudded into the wood of the railcar. Out of the smoke a rider appeared. Instinctively Hauck raised his rifle and returned fire. The rider fell from the horse and Hauck could see the look of surprise in his eyes. He had not expected any opposition. More shots rang out from the rear of the train, where Hauck could see another rider. From the trees by the side of the stream more horsemen broke cover, and as Hauck blasted away with his Winchester he saw spurts of flame come from the middle of the train. Riley had opened up on the outlaws. The carriages were still moving but eventually came to a halt just after the bridge where the railroad track took a slight incline.

The scene in front of Hauck was extremely confused. Shots were ringing out but it was difficult to make sense of what was happening for all the smoke swirling about. Seizing hold of a stanchion, Hauck placed his foot on a window ledge and, reaching up, hauled himself on to the roof of the train. Now he had a better idea of how the fight was progressing and it didn't look good. Horses and men were lying in the dust but there seemed to be many more riders than he had reckoned on and he could only surmise that the gang they had been following had been joined by other gunslicks.

Some of the gunmen had reached the train and were swinging themselves on board. There were shots from inside the carriage and the sound of screams. Doubled over, Hauck ran to the opposite end of the train where Birds Landing had taken up her position, shooting as he went. There were only four cars but it seemed like an aeon till he reached the end. He dreaded what he might find and felt an enormous sense of relief to see Birds Landing below him, firing rapidly at the oncoming riders. He jumped down beside her.

'Hauck!' she shouted. 'Look! There are too many of them!'

Hauck looked up and in the distance he could see more riders galloping towards them.

'Keep shootin'!' he shouted. 'But keep your head down!'

His rifle was empty and he drew his revolvers. He moved into the railcar. Two of the owlhoots were coming towards him and a bullet whined past his head. He fell sideways on to a vacant seat, fanning the hammer of his

Colt as he did so. Screaming passengers were squeezing themselves into the corners of the seats to try to avoid being hit. Both outlaws reeled back and collapsed to the floor. Hauck jumped up and ran forward, pushing past their dead bodies which were partially blocking the gangway. One of them he recognized. It was the young man who had joined their carriage in Prairie Junction. Hauck guessed it was he who had decoupled the cars.

When he reached the car he had occupied with Birds Landing and Riley, he was dismayed to see Riley lying back on the seat. When he reached him however, Riley waved him away. There was blood coming from a shoulder wound but it wasn't serious. Moving painfully, Riley began to fire out of the window again. Hauck turned his head and saw one of the migrants blazing away. There was another burst of fire from outside the train and then the sound of someone shouting. Hauck had run back outside and now he was amazed to see the remaining gunmen begin to ride away from the train, turning to fire as they did so. Some of them seemed to be aiming in another direction. Hauck was baffled till suddenly Birds Landing appeared by his side.

'Those riders!' she shouted breathlessly. 'They're not more outlaws. It's Marshal Harper with the posse!'

Hauck looked back. Birds Landing was right. It was the posse and it now broke into two, some members riding in pursuit of the remaining outlaws and the other group coming towards the train. Hauck jumped down, quickly followed by Birds Landing. The engineer was running towards them from one side while the posse rode up on the other. Some of the passengers, realizing that the shooting was over, were climbing from the train. As the posse approached Hauck recognized the marshal, who jumped down from his horse before it had fully stopped.

'Hauck!' he gasped. 'And Julia!'

Surprise was written all over his face and he looked even more nonplussed when he saw Riley coming towards them, clutching at his wounded shoulder. 'What in tarnation are you doin' on that train?'

Hauck grinned. 'Took you long enough to get here,' he said. 'That was cuttin' it mighty close!'

'Hell, we heard the shootin' and came right on over. We figured those owlhoots were somewhere around.'

When it came to reckoning up the damage, the outlaws had come out the worst. Four of them were dead and, apart from Riley, whose wound was not serious, only two of the passengers had sustained minor injuries. It was the element of surprise which had worked in Hauck's favour. Still, they had been lucky. A lot of the passengers were in a state of shock and it took some time to restore a semblance of normality.

By the time things had settled down and the engineer had recoupled the cars to the engine, the rest of the posse had returned, bringing with them a couple of wounded outlaws. It wasn't too clear how many had escaped but probably not more than half a dozen. Some of them must have joined the original group at Prairie Junction or another meeting point. As far as Hauck was concerned, they were of no account. It was the original group, who had carried out the massacre, that concerned him, and they had been dealt with. Although it was a very minor matter by comparison, the insult to Bird's Landing had been avenged. Even Riley, perhaps influenced in his attitude by his damaged shoulder seemed to be willing to call it a day.

'The rest of 'em won't cause no more trouble, leastwise not round these parts,' the marshal said. 'I reckon they've been taught a lesson. Besides, I ain't rightly sure I haven't exceeded my jurisdiction. That might be the last posse I ever ride.'

When the rest of the posse had returned and final preparations were being made for the train to continue on its way, Hauck noticed that the boxes he had observed being loaded earlier were being removed. Eventually the train started up to resume its interrupted journey, but Hauck and Birds Landing weren't on it. Instead they agreed to ride with the posse back as far as Prairie Junction where Riley and the two injured passengers could receive proper treatment.

When they arrived at Prairie Junction most of the posse elected to ride on. The marshal booked himself a night at the local hotel but couldn't persuade Hauck and Birds Landing to do likewise.

'Figure to spend the night under the stars,' Hauck said. 'Same as usual.'

Riley also took a room, opting to return to Scott Corner next day with the marshal. He would have carried on with the rest of the posse but his wound needed attention. At the hotel there was a note waiting for Hauck, inviting him and Birds Landing to a meal that evening in the hotel dining room.

'Well,' Hauck said. 'What's this all about? I ain't impressed with any cloak and dagger stuff.'

'There's only one way you'll find out,' the marshal said, 'and that's by bein' there.'

'Seems a bit odd. Especially comin' in the wake of everythin' else. Since you're booked into the hotel, would you like to come along?'

The marshal shook his head. 'I've had enough excitement for now,' he said. 'Reckon I'd do better to stay with Riley. Besides, I'm not invited.'

At seven that evening Hauck and Birds Landing turned up at the hotel and were shown to a corner table by a tired looking desk clerk. Hauck wasn't pleased by the fact that whoever had arranged the meeting was not there. He was pacified to a limited extent when a waiter turned up with drinks, including a bottle of bourbon which he left on the table.

Dusk had fallen and the restaurant

was lighted with shaded lamps, giving the place an intimate and relaxed atmosphere which belied its usual condition. A young couple with a child of about ten were sitting at one table when they came in, but soon got up and departed, leaving Hauck and Birds Landing in sole possession. They both took a drink, enjoying the taste after all the time they had spent on the trail. When he had downed his second glass Hauck turned to Birds Landing.

'I've about had it,' he said. 'Let's you and me make a move.'

Just as he was about to get to his feet a man appeared in the doorway and, hesitating for a brief moment, started towards them. Hauck watched the man approach. He wore a well-tailored suit of dark grey with a red waistcoat and bow tie. There was something about him that set Hauck on his guard.

'Good evening,' he said, taking a chair opposite to Hauck.

Hauck nodded in acknowledgement

and Birds Landing smiled.

'I understand you had some trouble earlier on the train,' the man said.

'It was nothin',' Hauck replied.

There was a spare glass and Hauck offered the man a drink. He took a long sip and then sat back in his chair.

'You're probably wonderin' what this is all about,' he said.

Hauck did not respond.

'Allow me to introduce myself. My name is Howard K Robbins and I act on behalf of Mr Kemble Rheinhardt.'

He had Hauck's attention now, although Hauck's features gave nothing away.

'I believe you are acquainted with Rheinhardt's Travelling Wild West Show?'

'Sure,' Hauck said.

'Mr Rheinhardt himself is currently overseeing some important business in Europe, otherwise he would have been here in person.'

Hauck was silent. Robbins glanced at

Birds Landing but her face was blank and her brown eyes seemed distant.

'Let me come to the point,' he said. 'You were recently in the employ of Mr Rheinhardt. In fact, you were one of the main contributors to the success of the show. I can tell you that you both made a deep and positive impression on Mr Rheinhardt. That's the main reason why he now seeks your assistance in a rather delicate matter.'

He paused, took another sip of bourbon, then resumed his discourse.

'As you may or may not know, Mr Rheinhardt is a widower. Since his wife died he has devoted himself to bringing up their daughter, Eustacia. She is now sixteen years old and until recently has been attending a school for young ladies in Boston.'

'Why do you say until recently?' Hauck interposed.

'Because about a week ago she disappeared from school and Mr Rheinhardt is only just in receipt of information as to her whereabouts. It seems she has been kidnapped and is currently being held for ransom, we think somewhere in the Blue Smoke Mountains.'

Hauck glanced at Birds Landing.

'Sure,' the man said. 'Nez Percé territory, or used to be. Mr Rheinhardt has done his research.'

'That's pretty specific,' Hauck said.

'Not so specific,' Robbins replied. 'The Blue Smokes cover a lot of territory.'

'But why there rather than anywhere else?'

'A friend of Mr Rheinhardt who once worked for Pinkerton's traced her as far as Pine Hollow. That much was quite easy.'

'Then why doesn't this friend carry on searchin' for the young lady?'

'For the simple reason that he's dead. He was shot. Might have been a coincidence. We think not. He sent a telegram before he died saying he was preparing to go up in to the mountains and wanting to know if Mr Rheinhardt was prepared to finance him in that enterprise.'

'You say she's being held for ransom,' Hauck said. 'That means you've heard from the kidnappers?'

'That is correct.'

'How much do they want?'

Robbins finished his drink before replying. 'That is the unusual part,' he said. 'They are not asking for payment in money. They want it in the form of stamps.'

'Stamps?' Hauck queried.

'In particular, a collection of United States Provisionals.' Seeing the puzzled look on the faces of Hauck and Birds Landing, Robbins continued: 'You may not realize it, but stamps are becoming quite valuable. Timbromania is a very popular pastime. Let me tell you about these particular stamps. Congress did not authorize the issue of stamps till 1847. Prior to that postmasters made provisional issues. Apparently these are becoming very collectable and people who know anything about such things regard them as being an excellent investment. Provisionals were issued in '45 and '46 by Baltimore, New York, New Haven, Annapolis, Battleboro and Lockport, among other places, and Mr Rheinhardt has a number of them.'

'But surely they could ask for money and then buy the things?'

Robbins shrugged. 'I guess so, but that would take a lot of time and effort. Seems like whoever has taken Eustacia is more interested in having a ready-made collection.'

'And you want Birds Landing and me to take the stamps and find the kidnappers?'

'That's about the size of it.'

'What else do we know about the kidnappers?'

'Nothing at all. The ransom note was posted in Pine Hollow.'

'Have you got it there with you?'

Robbins fished about in his jacket

pocket for a moment before coming up with a folded envelope which he passed across to Hauck. Hauck took a letter from it which he and Birds Landing perused together.

'Good quality paper,' Robbins said. 'It seems it was done on a new Oliver typewriting machine.'

'Doesn't say anythin' about arrangements for makin' contact.'

When Hauck and Birds Landing had finished reading it, Hauck handed the letter back to Robbins. There was a pause.

'Well,' Robbins said at length, 'what do I tell Mr Rheinhardt? Are you willing to take on this assignment?'

Hauck and Birds Landing exchanged glances. 'We're headed west anyway,' Hauck replied. 'Guess it ain't likely to take us too much out of the way.'

He rose to his feet. Birds Landing followed and they began to move away from the table.

'Haven't you forgotten something?' Mr Robbins called. Hauck turned back.

60

'I haven't said anything about remuneration.'

Hauck hesitated for a moment, as if trying to assimilate what Robbins had just said.

'Money,' Robbins added. 'And I can assure you Mr Rheinhardt is a most generous man.'

'How do we recognize Eustacia?' Birds Landing said.

Robbins looked confused. 'I'm sorry,' he said. 'I almost forgot.' He reached into his pocket again and this time came up with a photograph. Birds Landing stepped over and took it.

'Have those stamps ready by tomorrow early,' Hauck said.

They left the dining room, leaving Robbins sitting at the table. The waiter came up.

'I'm sorry,' Robbins said, 'but it looks as though my companions have other business. I'm afraid I'll be ordering for only one.'

* * *

Early next morning Hauck and Birds Landing returned to the hotel in order to say their goodbyes to Riley and the marshal. Riley's wound was little more than a burn and after a good night's rest he was in a better frame of mind. Nothing could undo the pain and misery of his parents' deaths but he had the consolation of having dealt with their killers and now all he wanted to do was to get back to Scott Corner and Hester.

'Thanks again for everything you've done,' he said, and metaphorically puffing out his chest, added: 'It was a pleasure to ride with you.'

The marshal shook hands with Hauck and Birds Landing. He didn't refer to the matter of the meeting with Robbins at the hotel; he seemed content to let that affair, whatever it involved, take its own course.

'If you're ever back this way,' Riley concluded, 'there'll always be a place for you at the farm.'

'Same goes for Scott Corner,' added

the marshal. 'Reckon the town owes you a debt for helpin' clean out that scum.'

The marshal and Riley swung into their saddles and rode slowly away. Just at that moment Robbins appeared. He looked flustered as he handed an envelope over to Hauck.

'Remember those stamps are valuable,' he said. 'Guard them closely.'

Hauck tucked the envelope away in an inner pocket. 'We'll be in touch,' he said.

'What's your plan? The easiest way to get to Pine Hollow would be to take a train best part of the way.'

'Guess that makes sense,' Hauck said, 'but I figure I've had enough of trains. Saw plenty of 'em back East.'

Hauck and Birds Landing climbed into leather and walked their horses down the quiet street. Hauck didn't mention that he had another reason for not taking the train. He and Birds Landing had recognized the picture of Miss Eustacia. She had been among the migrants heading for Cheyenne and Sioux City by way of Council Bluffs. Yet Robbins had told them she had been traced as far as Pine Hollow. Whatever hand Robbins was playing, it wasn't a straight one.

3

Council Bluffs, the western terminal of the Chicago & North Western Railway, connected with the Union Pacific by way of a great iron bridge over the Missouri river at Omaha. It was to the latter place that Hauck and Birds Landing made their way in hope of finding some trace of Eustacia Rheinhardt. There were two possibilities. Either she had left the train at this point or she had carried on westward on the Union Pacific. Being unsure what they were looking for, they first made their way to the crowded railway terminal and then to the migrant's lodging-house and outfitting shop adjoining it.

The shop was crowded and on the long counters across the room were piled clothes, boots and shoes, blankets, tin mugs, crockery and all the other things necessary for life on the frontier.

In the eating-room a cheap dinner was being served while a motley crowd drank at the bar. There were moose heads on the wall and a sign indicated the availability of lunch baskets.

'What do you reckon?' Hauck said. 'Show her picture around, see if anybody recognizes her?'

Birds Landing nodded, although they both knew it was a long shot. They returned to the outfitting shop and approached a man serving behind one of the counters.

'Seen this woman before?' Hauck enquired.

The man took the photo but quickly shook his head. They tried a few other people without success before making their way to the bar. Hauck pushed through the crowd and presented the picture to the bartender with the same result. The bartender pointed out to them a burly individual with bushy sidewhiskers.

'That's the superintendent. You could try him,' he suggested.

The superintendent was busy giving information to a bunch of weary-looking Germans and he seemed to be having problems making himself understood. When at last the conversation came to an end Hauck stepped in. The superintendent looked closely at the picture.

'What is your interest in this young woman?' he asked.

Hauck saw no reason to lie. 'She has gone missing,' he said. 'She could be in some danger.'

The man looked closely at Hauck, then his attention turned to Birds Landing. Something about them both seemed to reassure him.

'Well,' he said, 'it's kinda funny, but I do remember this young lady. She was in the company of some migrants and they asked about accommodation for one night. I thought it odd that they didn't travel straight on through, or at least make use of the facilities here. Instead they chose to move on to the Grand Central Hotel. Seemed a little extravagant to me, but then it takes all types.'

'Who was with her exactly?'

'Sorry, can't rightly answer that. Never took too much notice.'

'What about the man making the enquiries?'

The superintendent's brows wrinkled in concentration, but eventually he shook his head.

'Like I say, I never took much notice. Only remember the girl because she looked somehow different from a lot of the folk who pass through. She was a pretty girl — you can tell that from the likeness — but so are a lot of them. But not in the same way — she was somehow more delicate. And she had a strange look about her — sort of dreamy and vague.'

Hauck expressed his thanks and without further ado he and Birds Landing left the building and made for the centre of town. As its name implied, the Grand Central was easy to find. The entrance was large and the lobby impressive, with pillars, chandeliers and brocaded easy chairs beside low tables with bouquets of flowers. Two clerks were on duty behind the imposing desk. At Hauck's approach one of them detached himself and came forward.

'Can I be of assistance?'

Momentarily Hauck felt awkward. He and Birds Landing had been riding hard and he felt out of place.

'I'm looking for someone,' he said.

He explained the situation as briefly as he could, but when he asked to see the register the desk clerk was reluctant.

'I'm not sure I can do that, sir,' he said.

Hauck produced the picture of Eustacia Rheinhardt. 'Do you recognize her?' he asked.

The desk clerk looked, then shook his head.

'What about your friend?' Hauck said, indicating the other clerk.

The clerk was occupied in handing over the keys to one of the rooms to a man who had come in just ahead of Hauck and Birds Landing. After taking the keys, the man turned to Hauck, brushing against him.

'I hope you don't mind my butting in,' he said, 'but I couldn't help but overhear what you were saying. May I have a look at the picture?'

'Go ahead,' Hauck replied.

The man turned to the desk clerk who handed the likeness to him.

'Yes, I recognize this young lady,' the man said. 'She was with a party who booked in at the same time as me. They left the next morning. I saw them as I came out of the breakfast room. They seemed just like a normal family. They left in a carriage.'

The other clerk stepped forward. 'I can confirm that,' he said. He moved to the end of the counter and turned back a page of the hotel register. 'A Mr and Mrs Hamsun,' he said, 'with their daughter Daisy.'

'Thanks,' Hauck said. 'I sure appreciate your help.'

Hauck and Birds Landing decided to take a room for the night. There were a lot of puzzling questions and Hauck needed to think them through. He knew it would be Birds Landing who would come up with the likeliest answers.

'The thing that bothers me most,' he said, 'is how come Eustacia was traced to Pine Hollow and beyond, when we know now she's been here.'

'Maybe we're wrong. Maybe Daisy Hamsun just looks like Eustacia.'

'Maybe. Or maybe the Pine Hollow story is just that — a story to lead us way off the track.'

'I don't think so,' Birds Landing replied. 'That letter was postmarked Pine Hollow. I reckon the ex-Pinkerton man is real and that he got some sort of clue about where they were takin' her.'

'What about Robbins?'

'Robbins is behind the kidnap.' She said it with conviction. Hauck had faith in her insight.

'This is how I see it,' she continued.

'Robbins works for Rheinhardt. For some reason he decided to use his position to arrange the kidnap of Eustacia. Maybe he had a fall-out with Rheinhardt. More likely he's acting on behalf of someone else.'

'You figure that's the Pine Hollow connection?'

'Let's assume the ex-Pinkerton man exists. He found evidence that she was being taken to some place in the mountains. Robbins said he was killed. Why would Robbins lie about it? If that was the case, he must have been on to something pretty solid.'

'So what's Eustacia doin' round here?'

'She's being taken by a roundabout route. Throw anybody lookin' for her off the scent. We happened to be in Prairie Junction at the right time.'

Hauck was taking in what she was saying. 'Hey,' he said suddenly. 'You don't suppose those outlaws knew about it somehow? Maybe they attacked the train not so much because they figured it was carryin' loot as because they knew Eustacia was on board.'

There was a glint in Birds Landing's eyes. 'Could be,' she said.

'Another coincidence,' Hauck replied. 'We were chasin' after them for one reason; they were involved for another.'

'What do we do now?'

'Whoever Mr and Mrs Hamsun are, they ain't goin' to be travellin' by train. Besides, if they had rebooked through on the Union Pacific, the superintendent would have said something.'

'If he remembered.'

'He remembered Eustacia arrivin'. He didn't say anything about her returnin' to the station. Neither did anyone else we spoke to.'

'OK, we could be all wrong, but I guess what we have to do now is head for Pine Hollow. We could go by train, get there ahead of them.'

Hauck considered the suggestion. It made sense, but on the other hand they would have a better chance of coming up with the kidnappers if they followed their trail. Who would they look for in Pine Hollow?

'It could be a hard ride,' Hauck said. 'Especially if any of those outlaw varmints are left to follow along too.'

'What does Robbins get out of all this?'

'Who knows? Presumably he gets some kind of pay-off from whoever is behind it all and wants those stamps. Maybe the stamps are only part of it and once they get them they'll ask for more. Perhaps there were things in those boxes too. Maybe it's more personal.'

'You mean Robbins might have a grudge against Rheinhardt?'

'It could be an explanation. Let's face it; we're workin' in the dark. We'll just have to play it as it comes.'

The night was clear and below where they stood on the balcony of their room the lights of the town, clinging to the western bluff of the Missouri, twinkled. Looking further, they could see the river glinting in the starshine and

74

beyond that the dark prairie. The sound of a shunting train reached their ears. Birds Landing moved up close to Hauck.

'Let's go to bed,' he whispered.

The next morning they collected their horses from the livery stable. The ostler was a grizzled individual with a face like a scythe.

'You wouldn't have sold or hired any horses recently?' Hauck asked.

'Nope,' the man replied.

It was a long shot. It was unlikely the Hamsuns or their supporters wouldn't have had everything arranged well in advance. They swung their horses round and set off down the street. It was busy with a crowd of people and carriages, but soon they had left the place behind them. After a time they could see the silvery line of the Platte River to the south, running slowly between dark bluffs. Otherwise the country lay vast and open before them.

It seemed impossible that they might come across their quarry in all that emptiness, but if anyone could track them down Hauck had reason to know that it was Birds Landing. He was a good tracker himself but most of what he had learned he had learned from her. In any event, they knew where they were heading. If they hadn't sighted Eustacia before then, they would do so in the Blue Smoke Mountains.

★   ★   ★

Further ahead of them Miss Eustacia Rheinhardt was having the time of her life. Since the two people she knew as Uncle Roy and Aunt Edwina had collected her from school, life had been one grand adventure. First the trip from Boston and then the railroad journey, and now she was doing what she liked best of all — riding. Having grown up with the horses in her father's Wild West Show she was a very good rider. They had bought her a beautiful grey gelding she called Cloud and now she had the freedom of the open plains in which to ride him.

She had only one regret, and that was that her father, away in Europe, could not be with them. It was a grand adventure they were embarked on, going west all the way to the mountains. She felt like one of the pioneers who had crossed the continent in covered wagons before the advent of the railway. It wasn't so long ago either.

She had felt a little sorry for some of the latter day emigrants she had met with in Prairie Junction and Omaha. And, good gracious, they had even been attacked by outlaws! She hadn't liked that one bit, but what an experience to tell her friends about when she returned East. Now the sun was lowering towards the western horizon and she guessed they would soon be setting up camp for the night. Presently her uncle pointed towards a bunch of cottonwoods on their right.

'There'll be water near by,' he said.

When they had seen to the horses she sat back and watched as the people she called her uncle and aunt built a fire and prepared a meal. She had known Roy and Edwina Hobbs on and off for a long time and felt comfortable with them. Her father had employed them many times down the years; they came and went but always turned up again at some point. She guessed Uncle Roy was about forty but he was still good-looking. He had worked on a lot of ranches. At various times he had been a bronc twister, breaking raw horses into good saddle stock. It was hard, dangerous work and it was beginning to tell on him.

Aunt Edwina was slightly younger. She was thin and wore her hair short but they still made a handsome couple. Eustacia didn't know a lot about Aunt Edwina other than that she was quite willing to have knives thrown at her or have a cigarette shot from her mouth in the Wild West show. She was pretty handy with a gun herself. She was also a good cook and by the time they had finished eating Eustacia was full. She lay back and looked at the stars.

'Tell those stories to me again, Uncle Roy.'

Uncle Roy had produced a pouch of tobacco from his saddle-bags and he and Aunt Edwina were enjoying a smoke.

'Well,' Uncle Roy began, 'you see that group of stars up there? That's the Big Dipper. But for the Sioux, it's a great watering hole right in the middle of the Happy Hunting Ground.' He pointed elsewhere. 'That bright swath is the Milky Way. For the Sioux it is the pathway of the spirits. No one knows where their journey will lead them, but each star is a campfire blazing in the sky to mark their way.'

'So they could be looking down on us just like we are looking up at them?'

'I guess so.' He paused and reached into his pocket. 'Take a look at this,' he said.

He handed something across to her. In the dancing light of the fire she could see it was a round stone with a series of spots near its centre.

'Picked it up one time out on the prairie,' he said. 'It's a meteor stone but the Indians believe it is the shade of a star come back to where it came from.'

'I like that idea better,' Eustacia said.

'Keep it,' Roy said. 'Maybe it'll be lucky.'

'Are you sure? Oh, thank you.'

Roy reached out to pour an extra mug of coffee from the pot that was suspended above the flames, glancing across at Edwina as he did so. He thought he detected a look about her which told him she was as uncomfortable about what they had done as he was. When Robbins had suggested the kidnap, it hadn't seemed like a bad idea. With him and Edwina playing a central part, the girl's safety seemed assured. Now he wasn't so certain. Her life had already been put at risk on the train. That hadn't been part of the plan.

The man who had originated the whole kidnapping affair was Cullen

Dement, but what did they really know about him?

Only that he was a collector and lived as a recluse somewhere in the Blue Smoke Mountains. There had been paintings in those boxes, but it was apparently the stamps he was really after and willing to pay for. Could they trust an eccentric such as he seemed to be? They would have to do so if they wanted their payoff, a payoff which would allow Roy to cease putting his body at risk time and again and let his wife live a normal life, not the life of a vagabond . . . They would have enough to buy a little spread. The girl would know nothing about it; why, she was even enjoying it. In the firelight he could see the lines drawn about his wife's face. She deserved better.

They had been sitting quietly. Now Eustacia rose, came over to where he sat on the opposite side of the fire and kissed him on the cheek. She turned to Edwina and did the same.

'Goodnight,' she said, 'and thank you again.'

'I think I'll be turning in too,' Edwina responded.

Uncle Roy remained seated by the flames, his mind turning over and over the situation in which they now found themselves. The fire blazed up once and then died down. A wind had arisen and shook the leaves of the cottonwood trees. Suddenly he tensed. He thought he had heard something. Scarcely breathing, he listened intently. Was it simply the wind or was it something else?

Swiftly but silently so as not to disturb the others he got to his feet, drawing his gun as he did so. Something glistening caught his eye but it was only a reflection in the placid waters of the pool. The horses were quiet. They gave no indication of having detected anything.

Concentrating his attention, he listened again until he was assured that he had been mistaken. He had taken a step back towards the fire when out of nowhere something struck him like a thunderbolt. His head exploded into pain and he had the briefest glimpse of someone standing behind him with a raised rifle butt before he descended into a black night of unconsciousness.

When he came round the stars were fading and the sky was beginning to lighten in the east. He couldn't think for a moment where he was and then memory began to return at the same time as a pounding pain in his head. He attempted to sit up but his head felt as though it would burst. He sank down again with a groan and lay still for a while before trying again. This time he succeeded first in getting to his knees and then raising himself to his feet. He glanced around. The fire had gone out and only a few still smouldering embers remained. His senses returned and he looked about him for Eustacia and his wife. There was no sign of them or the horses. The place was deserted.

Staggering a little, he began to walk

around the campsite. It didn't take long for him to find the footprints of the intruder. There was only one set of them. He must have left his horse somewhere further off. The fact that he had taken the horses suggested there were more people involved, and the two women being gone meant that their capture had been the objective of the plot.

Putting his hands to his bent head, he cursed himself for not having been more careful. He had imagined the worst part of the whole affair would be in the towns and travelling on the railroad. He was comfortable in the wilderness and, feeling at home, had dropped his guard.

Still muttering beneath his breath, he staggered to the watering hole and splashed his way in. He lay in the water and dipped his head beneath the surface. It was cold and refreshing and his head began to feel a little better. There was a bad wound to the back of his skull where he had been slugged.

Blood had congealed but now it began to bleed again.

He came out of the water, took his bandanna and held it against the wound. He began to take stock of the situation. His position wasn't a good one. Without a horse he would be lucky to survive. Yet he couldn't remain where he was. He needed to get on the trail of whoever had taken Eustacia and Edwina. Who could it be? He wondered whether Robbins might be involved in some way.

He didn't trust Robbins. Never had. There was something about him which raised his hackles. But in what way could Robbins hope to benefit? Besides, Robbins was somewhere back in Prairie Junction. It was absurd. But somebody was in the know and expected to benefit by kidnapping Eustacia. Again he felt a powerful sense of guilt. Wasn't that just what he had done? He tried to convince himself that in his case it was different but it wasn't very effective.

At last he gave up thinking and

resolved to act. Maybe that way he could assuage his guilt. He took a few last gulps of water, put out the remnants of the campfire and started walking.

It was easy to follow the trail left by the horses. The imprints of one were more evident than the others and he guessed that two persons had ridden it. Whoever had taken Eustacia had probably seated her on its back and then swung up behind her. The sun had come up now and the morning was quickly getting warmer. Whoever had slugged him had taken his guns. That he had not bothered to kill him was something to be thankful for. Maybe one of the women had woken and disturbed him. More likely his attacker had just assumed that without a horse or provisions he would die soon enough anyway, which he was very likely to do.

He continued to walk, following the tracks till he came to a place where whoever had taken Eustacia had met up with some other riders. He reckoned there were four of them in all, including the man who had bushwhacked him. They had ridden away in a south-westerly direction. Looking up, he could see nothing that way except the never-ending, undulating prairie.

It was a grim prospect and for a moment he pondered whether to return to the waterhole. If only he had some means of carrying water, but the canteens had gone along with everything else. There was no point in thinking that way. After taking another close look at the evidence presented by the flattened grass, he started on again.

★   ★   ★

Hauck and Birds Landing had been riding at a steady pace for most of the day, stopping from time to time to rest the horses, making camp towards noon to eat and drink. They were looking for a good place to set up camp for the evening when suddenly Birds Landing pointed ahead.

'There's something over there!' she said.

Hauck looked but could see nothing. They drew to a halt, and after producing a pair of field glasses Hauck took a look in the direction she had indicated. Then he handed them to her.

'Somebody lying on the ground,' he said. 'Looks like a man. He's probably dead.'

She shook her head. 'He's alive. I see movement. He's breathing.'

The figure was a long way off. For all his acute senses Hauck would probably have missed that. He raised the glasses to his eyes once more.

'Still can't make much of it,' he said.

She looked at him. There was a hint of relief in her eyes.

'At least it ain't Eustacia,' he confirmed.

They turned their horses and started riding towards the man. At times the figure was partly concealed by dips and rises in the ground. Hauck was on the alert for trouble but the land was too open to conceal anybody and they had not sighted any horses. As they came over one last rise they were surprised when the man unexpectedly rose to his feet and began to wave. Hauck reached for his gun but it was soon evident that he would not need it. The man was unarmed and looked in a bad way. Coming up to him, Hauck slid from the saddle. Before he could say anything the man sighed deeply and began to laugh.

'Man!' he said. 'Am I glad to see you.'

Birds Landing, seeing his condition, had approached with a canteen of water in her hand. The man sank to his knees and she raised his head so that he could drink some of the precious liquid.

'Don't take too much at once,' she said. 'A few sips at a time.'

Hauck looked about him. There was a trail leading to and from where the stranger was lying. When the man had drunk as much as Birds Landing figured it was wise to give him, he looked up.

'Better introduce myself,' he said. 'The name's Hobbs, Roy Hobbs.'

'John Hauck. And this is Birds Landing.'

Now that they had left the settlements behind Hauck had given up using her other name, Julia. Not that he ever made much use of it anyway.

'You seem to have a few problems,' Hauck said. He looked meaningfully at Birds Landing. 'Guess some explanations might be in order.'

★ ★ ★

It was late. They had eaten and Roy Hobbs seemed like a new man. He had spun Hauck and Birds Landing a yarn: that he had been travelling west to take up a job when he was set upon by outlaws. Birds Landing knew of a trading post not too far off where he could pick up a horse and supplies.

'Kinda funny,' Hauck commented.

'What do you figure they were after?'

Hobbs shrugged. 'They got my horse and equipment,' he said.

Hauck passed him his pouch of Bull Durham. For a while they lay quietly, all three of them smoking. When he had finished his cigarette Hobbs rose to his feet.

'Mighty grateful to you folk,' he said, 'but I'm bushed. Reckon I'll lay me down for the night.'

'Take a blanket from the pinto,' Hauck said.

Hobbs moved to a spot away from the flames of the campfire. After a time Hauck and Birds Landing could hear him snore.

'He's not telling the truth,' Birds Landing said.

'Yeah, that's what I thought.'

'There were seven horses. One was not much more than a pony and another carried more than one rider. Even making allowances, that's more than he accounted for.'

'You figure he knows something

about Eustacia?'

'Seems a bit of a coincidence otherwise. Besides, I think I recognize him.'

'Funny you should say that. I was beginnin' to have the same feeling.'

'I reckon he's been with the travellin' show. Looks a lot different with that beard and all, but I reckon it's the same man.'

'Hobbs,' Hauck mused. 'Don't recall the name, but that means nothin'. He could have a whole string of aliases.'

Birds Landing drew up her legs and feet in a squat.

'Leave it till the mornin',' Hauck said.

4

When morning came they made a good breakfast. Hauck explained about the trading post.

'You can take my horse. I'll ride with Birds Landing.'

'Sure appreciate it.'

'By the way,' Hauck added like an afterthought, 'what happened to Mrs Hamsun?'

The man was cool. He gave no real indication that he had been taken by surprise but Birds Landing noticed the slightest hesitation before his reply.

'Hamsun?' he repeated.

Giving himself time, Hauck thought. 'Your wife?'

'Hey, I never said nothin' about no wife. Anyway, the name's Hobbs. I don't know what you're talkin' about.'

Hauck paused. Then, 'I think you're lyin',' he said.

Hobbs instinctively reached for the gun that wasn't there. 'I appreciate what you done for me,' he said, 'but no man calls me a liar.'

Hauck shook his head in an exasperated way. 'Why not cut your losses,' he said, 'and tell us what you done with Eustacia Rheinhardt?'

This time the barb went home and it was clear the man was flustered.

'Just to make it a bit easier,' Hauck said, 'I'll tell you somethin' of what we know and then you can fill in the rest.'

Briefly and without going into any details, he outlined how he and Birds Landing had become involved. 'Now we may be a pair of old-timers,' he concluded, 'but we ain't stupid.'

Hobbs looked from one to the other. Then he realized that he was beaten.

'OK,' he said, 'I'll tell you what happened. Fact of the matter is, I'll be glad to get it off my chest.'

Hauck and Birds Landing listened attentively as he unburdened himself.

'We didn't mean Eustacia no harm,'

he concluded. 'It was Robbins's idea. I'll admit I was persuaded by the chance to get out of the rut me an' Edwina always seem to be in, but our first concern was for the girl. She knows and . . . ' he hesitated.

'Go ahead,' Hauck snapped.

'I was goin' to say she trusts us. Guess she was wrong about that. But we figured it would be better for us to take on the job of kidnappin' her than to let anyone else do it.'

Hauck heard him out. He wasn't sure how far to believe him about Robbins, but it made no difference. The man seemed genuinely contrite.

'So who's taken Eustacia now?' he asked.

Hobbs shook his head.

'Matter of fact, we got us some idea,' Hauck said.

'You were taking her as far as the Blue Smokes,' Birds Landing intervened. 'What did you intend doin' with her when you got there?'

'Look, I never thought it through. I

know we done wrong. But believe me, I wouldn't have done nothin' to hurt Eustacia.'

'What do you know about who's behind this plot? Robbins was givin' nothin' away when we spoke with him.'

'I don't know all the details, but I think it's somebody called Dement. I've come across him a couple of times.'

Hauck's brow lined with concentration. 'You know, I think I have too. Back when I was doin' some prospectin'. That name sure rings a bell. If he's who I think he is, I wouldn't put somethin' like this past him.'

'He's some kind of eccentric now. Lives alone some place hidden way up in the mountains and collects things.'

'What things?'

'Anything. Pictures, paintings, old manuscripts, pottery.'

'Stamps?'

'I guess so, if they're worth anythin'.'

Hauck kicked out the campfire. 'You must be worryin' about Edwina,' he said.

The man gave him a crestfallen look.

'OK,' Hauck said. 'Here's what we do. First we track down those outlaw scum and rescue Eustacia and your wife. We give the varmints what they're owed. When we've done that and Eustacia is safe we ride all the way to the Blue Smoke Mountains and pay Mr Dement a visit.'

'You missed out Robbins,' said Birds Landing.

'He'll get his turn,' Hauck said. He turned to Hobbs. 'You'd better just pray that no harm has come to Eustacia,' he added.

★   ★   ★

Two days had come and gone since Eustacia had been rudely awakened from her sleep and dragged screaming from the scene around the campfire. Confused and terror-stricken, she had called for Uncle Roy but he had not appeared. Instead, as she was man-handled towards the horses, Aunt

Edwina had woken and thrown herself upon the intruder. She had succeeded in dragging him down but he had hit her hard across the face, knocking her to the ground. She had seemed to be unconscious but, as he eventually succeeded in saddling the horses, she had struggled to her feet. Seeing that she could not stop him she had pleaded to be taken along with Eustacia. He had not objected.

Aunt Edwina had climbed into the saddle of her bay while he swung himself up behind Eustacia on Roy's horse, leading the grey, Smoke, behind them. Before long they had met up with other riders and they had all ridden off together.

Now Eustacia had just awoken from a fitful, troubled sleep with a sense of pressure on her chest. It was the rough blanket one of the men had thrown across her. It was a small gesture of consideration that she was grateful for, especially as she had a feeling that he was the one member of the gang who so far had prevented anything worse happening to either of them. She lay on her back as tears began once more to flow down her cheeks. What had happened to Uncle Roy? Had they killed him?

She listened to the night and peered into the shadows beneath the willow brake. The wind had got up during the evening and the brush seemed to be filled with movement. Turning her head the other way she could just make out the figure of Aunt Edwina. She couldn't see any of the men who had taken them but she knew they were stationed near by. They knew that there was no chance of them escaping and they had not taken any particular precautions. Where were they taking her? She closed her eyes once more but it was a long time before sleep returned.

★　★　★

As soon as they came in sight of the trading post Birds Landing knew that

99

something wasn't right, even though the place gave an appearance of normality. It was a surprisingly large building with a yard in front and some trees behind. There were a couple of sheds and off to one side was a rough corral. There were too many horses in it.

'Over in the corner,' Hobbs said. 'Eustacia's pony.'

Hauck took out his field glasses and surveyed the scene. The horses in the corral looked as though they had been ridden quite recently. The yard in front of the building was churned up and there were horse-droppings.

'Looks to me like a heap of people just rode in.'

'It's gotta be those outlaw varmints.'

'Yup. Leavin' aside all the other evidence, the trail has led us right to it.'

'They didn't take much effort to clean up that camp we found this mornin'.'

'They seem pretty sure of themselves.'

Hauck turned to Birds Landing. 'Seems like even after what happened in Scott Corner and on the train, they still ain't learned nothin' yet. Maybe it's time we taught 'em another lesson,' he said.

They got down from the horses and hobbled them among some bushes.

'We got to get Eustacia and Edwina out before anythin' else,' Hauck said.

'They could be in one of those sheds,' Hobbs suggested.

'Yeah, it's a good chance. Leave this to Birds Landing.'

There wasn't a lot of cover between them and the trading post, but once Birds Landing had crept away neither Hauck nor Hobbs could see any sign of her. Stooping low, she made a wide circuit of the building which took her into the trees behind. She took her knife from its sheath, got down on her belly and began to slither towards the nearest of the outhouses. Upon reaching the back wall she listened carefully. There was no sound to indicate that the outhouse might be occupied. Gliding like a phantom to the front, she raised herself up to peer through an uncurtained window. There was nothing inside but a lot of boxes containing what she guessed were supplies. She turned and made her way to the other shed.

As she got close the door suddenly opened and a man stepped out. He slammed the door behind him and slithered down on his haunches. Birds Landing seemed to have found what she was looking for but the man wasn't moving. He must be acting as guard. Silently and stealthily as fate she moved towards him, coming at him from the side. Slowly, slowly at first she made her approach.

The man, all unconscious of the danger, pulled out a pouch of tobacco and proceeded to roll himself a smoke. He glanced up and Birds Landing saw her chance. With the deadly impetus of a rattler she launched herself at the man and the next moment her knife sliced across his throat and he fell to one side, a look of surprise written across his features and his hand still grasping the cigarette.

Quickly Birds Landing got to her feet and, stepping over the prostrate form of the guard, pushed at the door. It wasn't locked. Once inside it took no time for her eyes to adjust to the gloom. She could see at once the two women, who were clinging to each other in fright against the back wall.

'Do not be afraid,' she said, and then to reassure them she mentioned the name of Roy Hobbs.

'Roy! Is he OK?' the older woman gasped.

'No time for explanations. Follow me.'

Without waiting, Birds Landing stepped through the doorway and after a moment the others followed. Eustacia gave a little cry of fright as she saw the dead man sprawled in the dust. Birds Landing grasped her and they all began to run towards the trees at the back. Someone must have heard her because the door of the trading post swung open and a number of men came running out.

They were not far from the shelter of the trees when someone shouted and a shot rang out. It must have been meant as a warning because there was no follow-up. Instead there came the pounding of boots as the men turned and ran towards them, calling on others to join them in the hunt. More men came out of the building and from behind the corral a few others appeared, attempting to cut off their avenue of escape.

Birds Landing could have got away with ease. Despite her years she could still run faster than most men but now she was hampered by the other two women. Shouting at them to carry on into the trees, she turned to face their pursuers, pulling a gun from her waistband.

A shot whistled close by. She took only a moment to take aim before pulling the trigger and the leading figure of the group that had emerged from behind the corral fell to the ground as blood spurted from his chest. She fired again and another man went spinning backwards. There were two others and another effect of the shot was to halt them in their tracks. Birds Landing turned to run as the men recovered themselves, and as she made for the trees there came a loud crash of fire from her left.

The two men went down as Hauck and Hobbs burst into view on the appaloosa and the pinto, Hauck's pump-action .22 Winchester spitting out a deadly hail of lead while Hobbs fired away with Hauck's handguns. A fusillade of shots rang out from inside the trading post as whoever was left inside returned fire through the windows. The horses in the corral were rearing with fright and now they broke through the ill-repaired fences.

For a few moments there was a scene of complete confusion as they stampeded among the gunmen and a haze of smoke hung over the place. Birds

Landing was in amongst the trees and soon caught up with the others, urging them on. Branches caught at them and once Eustacia tripped over a tree root and fell badly. Edwina helped her to her feet and they ran on as the noise of battle rang out behind them.

Presently the rattle of gunfire diminished and then died away completely. Telling the other two to wait, Birds Landing made her way quickly but cautiously back through the trees. When she came out into the open it was to see Hauck and Hobbs rounding up the last of the outlaws who hadn't been killed. Although they had been well outnumbered, it was the element of surprise that had carried the day. As Hauck had commented, the gunslicks had been too casual, not anticipating that any rescue bid was likely to take place.

The problem arose as to what to do with them. There were two of them and an additional two slightly wounded. In the end Hauck decided to let them go. There didn't seem to be much alternative. First he removed their weapons, then he allowed them to take their horses from the corral. He provided them with water and supplies.

'Keep ridin',' he warned.

'It's more than the varmints did for me,' Hobbs remarked.

There was little danger of them causing any further disruption. This time they were demoralized. Among them was a man called Rascombe, the same one who had shown some sympathy towards Eustacia. Like Hobbs, he seemed to feel a certain shame at having been involved in taking Eustacia in the first place.

'How d'you get involved?' Hauck asked. 'Who was behind it?'

'I don't know much, but I heard talk of someone named Robbins. I figured we was after some boxed up loot. I didn't realize the young lady was involved.'

'The name Dement mean anythin' to you?'

'Dement? Nope. Any reason it should?'

'No particular reason. Me and Hobbs have come across him before. Seems like he's the person really responsible for all this.'

'Have you got anythin' else to go on?'

Hauck shook his head. 'Only that he's got some sort of set-up in the Blue Smoke Mountains.'

The man suddenly looked interested. 'The Blue Smokeys?'

'Nez Percé country.'

'Funny you should mention them,' the man said. 'I once rode with someone who always used to say he was gonna set up there real big one day when his ship came in. That's how he put it. Hey, I know I got my faults but he was one real mean coyote.' He looked at Hauck. 'This man Dement; by any chance does he collect things?'

Hauck eyed the man closely.

'I know it sounds strange, but this *hombre* I'm tellin' you about used to make a habit of it. He sure had some strange items: stuffed animals, things in jars. Apparently that was his job back East before he decided to head West and take up the owlhoot trail. Stuffed things. Like people wanted their dogs or cats preserved or maybe an old bird in a cage. A taxeedermatist I believe he said he was called.'

'Could be the same man,' Hauck said. 'Only now it's more collectable items; old books, old prints, paintings.'

'If it's the same *hombre* it makes no difference. He's still a number one ornery varmint.' He looked a little sheepishly at Hauck. 'Say, I know I got no right to ask this, but would you let me ride along with you?'

'Don't you want to catch up with your friends?'

'They ain't no friends of mine. I seen the light.'

'There's plenty of space for a man to ride,' Hauck said. 'But why would you want to ride with us?'

'You got me interested in this man Dement. He owes me. If it's the same

109

man, I'd sure like to catch up with him again.'

'If none of the others objects it's OK by me,' Hauck said.

★ ★ ★

Eustacia proved to be little the worse for her ordeal. Having Edwina along had made a big difference and although the outlaws had been unpleasant they hadn't offered her any worse treatment. Maybe the presence of Rascombe had made a difference. Maybe they were under orders not to offer her any violence. Whatever it was, once she had time to rest and recuperate she was OK once more. Hauck and Birds Landing had agreed not to say anything about the part Uncle Roy and Aunt Edwina had played in the episode.

It was agreed that they would take her as far as Pine Ridge, as had been the original intention. She wouldn't know that the whole affair had been anything other than a holiday, albeit one attended by some unfortunate consequences. What they would do with her there Hauck wasn't sure. That was something they could leave. The first thing would be to contact her father in Europe, but the problem was that his exact whereabouts were unknown.

The next day, as they were about to leave, they were surprised by the arrival of the owner of the trading post. He had been conducting some business with the Indians on the local reservation and remained in ignorance of what had occurred in his absence till he heard the story from Hauck. He had left someone to look after the store in his absence, who turned out to be one of the outlaw gang.

Not far behind him came a wagon and a party of three Sioux, two young men and an older man, come to pick up some supplies. Eustacia watched with fascination as they rode into the yard and entered the store, but they were not quite like the Indians of her imagination. They wore the same clothes as anyone else and there was little to distinguish them, apart from a feather one of them wore in his hat and the older man's hairstyle.

They came out of the shop, and began to load the wagon. Eustacia went off to see Edwina. Hauck continued watching them and his brows puckered with concentration. A strange, incredulous look came over his features. Birds Landing, coming up to him saw the intense look with which he was still regarding the eldest of the trio.

'What is it?' she asked.

'Look at that man,' Hauck said.

Birds Landing regarded the man closely. He was of about the same age as themselves or a little older. His face was lined with wrinkles and he wore his greying hair in two long plaits.

'What of him?' she asked.

'You wouldn't remember. You only met him once or twice, a long time ago. But you've heard me talk about him plenty. Unless I'm mistaken, that man is Otoktay.'

'Otoktay? Your old friend? But that was so long ago.'

'A long, long time,' Hauck replied. 'I haven't seen him for many years, but I'd swear that was him.'

★ ★ ★

Hauck's memory carried him back to the time when he had been a very young man, not even twenty before the War between the States. It was at the time he had first met Birds Landing. The wheel seemed to have come full circle. He had been fighting a band of outlaws then, alongside a group of goldminers to whom he had been delivering mail. It was a long story but in the course of it he had met the Sioux chieftain. He remembered how Otoktay had looked when he first met him. He was riding a white pony with a warpaint hand imprinted on its neck, wore a split-horn headdress and carried a lance decorated with eagle feathers. When he had ridden into the Indian village to meet up with him later they had smoked the peace pipe and sworn friendship. Otoktay had given Hauck the Sioux name of Cetanwakuwa.

'It mean attacking hawk. Let there be friendship between Otoktay and Cetanwakuwa, between Cetanwakuwa and Lakota people,' he had proclaimed, and Hauck had apologized for the behaviour of the outlaws who were their common enemy.

'Tell the chief that Hauck apologizes for actions of bad men. Those men are beyond the law. Hauck wages war against outlaws. Let Otoktay and Cetanwakuwa be united against bad men.'

★   ★   ★

In view of what had been happening since he and Birds Landing had left the Wild West Show, nothing seemed to have changed in that respect. Birds Landing's voice interrupted his reverie.

'There's only one way to find out.'

Hauck moved towards the group of Indians who seemed to have completed loading the wagon. As he approached the two younger men looked up but the older one carried on working. He was on the opposite side of the wagon as Hauck spoke.

'Otoktay!'

The man looked up across the wagon. 'Yes, what is it?' He spoke strongly accented English. 'Do you remember me?'

The Sioux paused in his work and looked at him again, continuing to stare for a few moments. Then the semblance of a smile parted his lips.

'Is it you, my old friend?' he said.

Hauck walked quickly round the back of the wagon and approached the Indian with his hand outstretched, palm uppermost.

'It's been a long time,' he said as they embraced.

When the first shock of recognition was over Hauck introduced Birds Landing.

'So, you are still together?' Otoktay said. 'That is good.' He turned to the two younger men. 'These are my nephews, Chankoowashtay and Ohanzee. And now tell me, what brings you here?'

It was much later when the wagon eventually departed. Hauck and his old friend had much to catch up on and neither of them was in any hurry. Only the two nephews began at last to show signs of impatience. Hauck watched the wagon as it rolled across the prairie for a long time before preparing to go back and rejoin the others. He felt an unwonted sadness. The old days had gone and things had changed so much. It was a different world and he felt less and less a part of it. Just then he heard footsteps approach. It was Birds Landing.

'Come on, John,' she said. 'Supper's ready.'

The next day they rode out, taking with them two spare horses. They were well provisioned and well rested. Hauck couldn't help thinking what an odd bunch they were: two old-timers, a girl, a couple of ex-kidnappers and a reformed outlaw. Life was strange. It led you in ways you'd never expected to go. There seemed to be something unreal about the way he and Birds Landing had got caught up in events since the day they had helped Riley with his broken-down buggy. It was all chance and coincidence. Life had seemed different in the old days. He glanced at Birds Landing. Yeah, she was real enough and always had been.

* * *

The morning passed and they stopped at noon. The air was warm and swarms of flies hung in clouds, attracted by the horses. Towards the end of the afternoon they saw ahead of them a creek bottom and they headed towards it. As they got closer Birds Landing pointed to something that her keen eyes had detected. Hauck could see nothing at first, then he saw that it was a horse, screened by the trees.

'Now who do you suppose that could be?' Hauck said.

'Could be more of those outlaw scum,' Hobbs suggested.

'I don't think so. They would have been more careful. Besides, we turned 'em loose without any irons.'

They rode a little further. 'Wait here,' Hauck said. 'Me an' Birds Landing will go on ahead.'

While the others sat their horses, Hauck and Birds Landing rode the rest of the way. Coming through the trees, they saw someone sitting with his back to them. Even before he turned his head it was perfectly obvious who he was.

'Otoktay!' Hauck breathed.

It was the old Sioux chief, but he looked different. In place of the routine attire of the previous day he was wearing a buckskin shirt decorated with intricate beadwork together with a breechcloth and leggings of tanned hide. On his head was a war bonnet of notched eagle feathers. For a few moments Hauck was reminded once again of the way he had looked when they first encountered one another. Hauck glanced at the horse. The dun-coloured mustang was brightly decorated with circles round its eyes, yellow arrow heads on its hoofs and purple thunder stripes on its front legs. A medicine bag had been woven into the bridle and coup feathers braided into the forelock and tail. What struck Hauck the most was the upside-down hand-print on the horse's chest. It was the most prized symbol a warrior could use and it signified a do-or-die mission.

'I knew you would come this way,' Otoktay said.

Hauck dismounted and as Otoktay rose to his feet, they embraced. Afterwards Hauck took a step back to admire his friend in all his finery.

'If this was twenty years ago, I'd think you were goin' into battle,' Hauck said.

A smile spread across the Indian's face. 'Some government agency somewhere probably wouldn't like it,' he replied.

'So what's the reason?'

'I've had enough of living on the reservation,' Otoktay said, and then breaking into a former manner of speech, 'Otoktay ride with his old friend Cetanwakuwa.'

'I'd be glad to have you along. But I don't want to go frightening the ladies.'

Again the old Indian smiled. 'Never figured to ride all the way to the Blue Smokes like this,' he said. He glanced at the sky. 'It's gettin' along. Why don't the rest of you ride right on in and make yourselves comfortable for the night.'

It seemed a reasonable proposition so Birds Landing went to get the others. When she saw the Indian chief in his ceremonial gear Eustacia was very impressed and even more so when she learned he would be coming along with them. She had already taken to him on meeting him at the trading post. Hauck was pleased to be reunited with his old friend but it seemed to him that now, more than ever, they were a strangely assembled company.

Otoktay seemed to be satisfied that he had made his point and before long was back in his customary clothes. He had mellowed over the years and adapted the white man's ways. Still, Hauck was troubled. He realized that although the old Indian might make light of his behaviour, the underlying motive was real enough. Otoktay had been in earnest when he dressed in the traditional way and drew those symbols on his horse. As far as the old chief was concerned, he was on a deadly quest, and Hauck had learned to trust the red man's intuition.

5

High and almost inaccessible in the Blue Smoke Mountains Cullen Dement had built his retreat. His ranch-style house was situated in a small hidden valley surrounded by lofty peaks and protected behind by an impregnable snow-capped mountainside. Dement had discovered the place by chance during the long-ago days of his youth when he had come to the area as a prospector. Finding no success, he had struck further and further into the high peaks, following disused trails that no one but Indians had used in the past.

One morning he had entered the narrowest of canyons. It seemed to end in a dead wall of rock but, skirting it a little way, he found another opening. It was too narrow for his horse but something about it drove him on. Squeezing his way through, he had unexpectedly been rewarded by his first sight of the hidden grassy bowl surrounded by mountains. He could see at once its possibilities. Protected by the peaks and many hundreds of feet lower than the surrounding terrain, it offered a haven of temperate seclusion.

At first he had considered the possibility of ranching in this high spot. The grass was rich and thick and could provide better feed than the lower slopes or even the prairie lands. A stream ran through the valley so there would be no problems about water. It was an attractive possibility but he soon rejected it. He had some experience of ranching and it wasn't really for him.

The hidden valley offered other options, above all the possibility of one day returning to live there away from the hurly-burly of life's struggle. That was really why he had come to the mountains in the first place. It wasn't so much the prospect of gold as the allure of the empty remote spaces. He vowed then that he would first enter that struggle, make his pile, and then return. It might take time, but if there was one distinctive thing about Dement, it was that he generally got his way.

Now he leaned on the veranda of his ranch house, looking out across the valley and taking pleasure from the fact that it was all his. No one was likely to make his way to that remote spot and just in case anyone might be tempted by rumours of his treasured collections he had plenty of protection from his gang of resident gunslicks.

As he mused his eyes were attracted to a group of three riders approaching from the direction of the mountains. They came on at a fast pace and were soon swinging down from their saddles in front of him.

'Boss, looks like there might be a little problem.'

Dement looked from his foreman Jeb Doolan to the other ranch hand. The third man, who looked rough and unkempt, he didn't recognize.

'Yeah? What's this all about?'

'Go ahead,' Jeb said, addressing the unkempt man. 'Tell Mr Dement what you told us.'

The man hesitated, as if not sure where to begin. Then he cleared his throat.

'I bin ridin' hard to get here,' he said. 'Thought the best thing I could do would be to tell you what happened.'

Dement eyed him suspiciously; a slight sneer curled up the corner of his mouth.

'If you have information useful to me,' he said, 'you'll be rewarded.'

'Thanks, Mr Dement.'

'Get on with it then,' Dement snapped.

'Well, it's about that young Miss Rheinhardt.'

At the mention of the name Dement seemed to straighten and his attention was firmly fixed on what the newcomer was saying.

'I was part of the group organized by Mr Robbins to kidnap her. It went fine. We left her with the Hamsuns at

Omaha. I figured my part was done but before I had time to leave I heard that Mr Robbins was in town. There was a bunch of people in the hotel lounge. Mr Robbins had maybe been drinkin', I'm not sure. He seemed to be enjoyin' himself. Anyway, when things had quieted down me an' him ended up havin' somethin' to eat in the hotel dining room.

'It was then that he let on that he had put one over on you, Mr Dement. I didn't know what he meant. Gradually, though, he let on that he had taken on his own bunch of hired guns to take Eustacia. There had been some sort of incident involving a train which had been unsuccessful but now he had her. Seems like he was double-crossin' you, Mr Dement. Figured he could get more out of takin' the girl for himself than he could simply deliverin' her to you.'

As the man progressed with his tale Dement's face had clouded and he looked grim.

'Why should I believe any of this?' he rapped.

'What reason would I have to make it up and then come all this way?'

Dement was thinking fast. The man's story had a ring of truth about it. He had never fully trusted Robbins. It seemed like the sort of trick he might pull.

'Take him to the bunkhouse,' he said at length to Jeb Doolan. 'Get Moose to give him something to eat.' He turned to the unkempt rider. 'You'd better not be lyin',' he said. 'Either way, I'll find out.'

* * *

After talking through the situation several times especially with Birds Landing and Otoktay, Hauck had come to a similar conclusion. At first he had been tempted to think that the intervention of the outlaw gang had simply been a coincidence. Now he was beginning to think otherwise and it seemed not unreasonable that Robbins might be behind it.

'But what would he have to gain?' Otoktay asked. 'He already had Eustacia.'

'He also had the stamps before he handed them over to Hauck,' Birds Landing commented.

'My guess is he just got too greedy and he also got a bit too clever. He could maybe have avoided hiring anybody to do his dirty work but then it would have been obvious if Eustacia disappeared that he was behind it. By having Eustacia taken by someone else he diverted suspicion away from himself. It was a ruse designed to throw Dement off the track.'

'He must have a healthy respect for this person Dement,' Otoktay said.

'Yeah, if he was prepared to go to those lengths to distance himself.'

Rascombe had sat quietly during this interchange. Now he looked over at the others.

'Dement is a very dangerous man,' he

said. 'If he's the same man I'm thinkin' of, he won't let anythin' stand in his way. If I were Robbins I wouldn't sleep easy.'

Hauck nodded. 'And since we've got Eustacia, I guess the same goes for us.'

'How would Dement know what's happened?' Hobbs queried. 'Remember, he's all the way to the Blue Smokies.'

'Believe me, Dement has his ways. His tentacles extend pretty far and wide.'

'The way things stand, we'd better be extra cautious,' Hauck said. 'Remember, we could have Robbins as well as Dement to contend with. The quicker we hit Pine Hollow and make sure Eustacia is safe the happier I'll be.'

Later, when they had set up camp for the evening, Birds Landing approached Hauck with another suggestion.

'We could go back to Omaha,' she said. 'Or even Scott Corner. We could leave Eustacia with Wendell Riley. I'm sure he would be happy to look after her till her father can be traced.'

'I've thought about it,' Hauck said, 'and it makes a lot of sense. But we've come a long way. It's almost as easy to get to Pine Hollow as to return to Scott Corner. I don't know about you, but I got a feelin' I'd like to meet up with this Dement.'

He looked closely at Birds Landing. She looked relieved.

'I figure you got a hankerin' for those mountains,' he said.

She laughed, sounding surprisingly young. 'West is where we both want to go,' she replied. 'Remember?'

As they progressed the old Sioux warrior Otoktay seemed to be by turns elated and crestfallen. He was content to be travelling with Hauck and Birds Landing. For too long he had been confined in the reservation. Now, whatever the consequences, he felt free. But he remembered the time when the open plains had been filled with buffalo. Now there was little enough of either freedom or buffalo.

Like most of his contemporaries they were gone together with the traditional ways of life. He was a misfit.

Looking across at Hauck and his woman the shadow of a smile crossed his features. They were misfits too. They were out of time, but this was like the old days. What did it matter if it was only a reprise, that it couldn't last? They were riders on the wind. Their day was almost over; the day now belonged to Eustacia. The Sioux chief had struck up an understanding with the young girl and had even given her an Indian name — Magaskawee.

'That sounds nice,' she said, 'but what does it mean?'

The old Indian thought for a moment. 'It means graceful,' he said. 'Graceful, like an antelope.'

'Like Birds Landing?' Eustacia replied.

'Yes, like Birds Landing. She too is like an antelope, but an antelope with horns of steel and hoofs of fire.'

One evening Eustacia showed the old

Indian the stone which Uncle Roy had given her.

'You need something to keep it in,' Otoktay said.

He went to his horse and returned carrying a small bag made of buckskin leather with a long leather fringe and stitching of coloured porcupine-quill pieces.

'There, that is now your medicine bag. You can put the stone into it.'

Eustacia did as he suggested. 'Can I put other things into it?' she asked.

'Of course. That is what it is for. It is for anything that becomes important to you. You will know what they are. From now on the medicine bag will protect you.'

* * *

Back in Omaha Robbins was in something of a quandary. He had just heard the story of what had happened with Eustacia from one of his erstwhile gang of kidnappers whom he had met in the saloon. Now he was trying to work out what his next move should be. He considered what the chances were of recapturing Eustacia but they were not good. It seemed he had missed out on that option. When he looked at things in the cold light of day, it seemed he had maybe mismanaged the whole affair. Once Dement heard about things he would be very likely to put two and two together and he wasn't the sort of person to leave it go.

Thinking hard about the possibilities, it seemed to Robbins that the best thing he could do would be to cut his losses and settle for having the stamps. They were worth something. A thin smile spread across his features. At least he hadn't been fool enough to let the stamps out of his grasp. The stamps he had given Hauck had been worthless. After all, what did he know about stamps? He reached into an inner pocket of his jacket where he kept his wallet and drew out the precious United States Provisionals. Seemed like people would be prepared to shell out good money for practically anything. The best thing would be to catch a train back to Chicago and then disappear.

Having made the decision he proceeded to act on it. After all, there was no point in delay. The sooner he vanished from the scene the better. Quickly he began to pack the items he would need into a portmanteau. He was almost finished when there was a knock on the door. He slid the portmanteau under the bed and stepped forward to answer it.

'Who is it?' he called.

'Room service.'

Robbins hesitated. He hadn't asked for room service. Then he shook his head. He was getting nervous. There was no reason for it. He was well ahead of the game. He was letting his anxieties get the better of him.

'Just a moment,' he called.

He straightened his tie and waistcoat and opened the door. There was a man outside. Something about him tugged at Robbins's memory, but he couldn't place him. Then too late he realized that whoever the man was, he wasn't room service. Before he could do anything the man had pushed him back into the room and shut the door behind him.

'What do you think you're doing?' Robbins demanded.

'Where are the stamps?' the man replied.

Robbins gave him an uncomprehending look.

'I want the stamps,' the man said. He put his hand into his pocket and produced an envelope. 'Look in there,' he said.

Robbins opened the envelope. Inside were the stamps he had given Hauck.

'I met your go-between in the foyer of the Grand Central,' the man said. 'It was an easy enough matter to steal these. All I had to do was brush up against him.'

'I don't know what you're talking

about,' Robbins stuttered. 'Who are you? Some kind of petty thief?'

'Never mind that. Just tell me what you've done with the stamps. The real ones.'

Robbins was desperate. He decided it was no use to pretend ignorance.

'All right,' he said, 'you have me. I've got the stamps inside my jacket pocket.'

'Let me see them.'

Trying to control his trembling hand, Robbins reached inside his jacket. Hidden in a holster beneath his armpit he carried a derringer. Slowly he drew it out. Sweat had appeared on his brow. With a swift movement he withdrew his hand but the stranger was too quick. Before Robbins could fire a gun had appeared in the man's hand. Robbins sank to the floor as a bullet caught him square between the eyes. For the briefest of moments he felt the stranger's hand search his pocket before he succumbed to darkness and oblivion.

* * *

The first sign Hauck's party had that they were approaching Pine Hollow was when they caught sight of smoke from passing trains, still a good way ahead of them. As they rode along the distant barking of a dog reached their ears and somewhere a rooster crowed. The town itself consisted mainly of a block-long main street of frame buildings which ran parallel to the rails. The rest of the town extended westward from this: stores, saloons, gambling dens. On the north side of the tracks were the station, section house and a number of buildings which Hauck assumed were the homes of its permanent residents. It was fairly unprepossessing. Behind it, however, were the foothills of the Blue Smokes and beyond them the high peaks and untrodden heights where Dement had his secret domain.

After leaving their horses at the livery stables they made their way to the biggest hotel, the Exchange, where they intended to eat and book rooms for Eustacia, Hobbs and Edwina. It was Hauck's plan to leave Eustacia with the couple she still called her aunt and uncle when the time came for the rest of them to head into the mountains. He had talked it over with Birds Landing whose opinion he trusted implicitly and she agreed with him that it would be safe to do so. Hobbs had proved himself since they had rescued him and it was clear that his contrition and that of Edwina was sincere.

When Hauck broached the matter to them, they were anxious to assure him that Eustacia would be safe. Hobbs, however, was adamant about accompanying the others into the Blue Smokes when the time came.

'We both feel ashamed of what we did,' he said. 'The only way I can feel good about myself again is if I catch up with Dement and see that he gets what he deserves.'

Hauck nodded. 'I can see that,' he

replied. 'You're welcome to string along.'

That first evening they all ate in the hotel dining room, except for Otoktay who felt uncomfortable being indoors and sought instead the open spaces outside of town. When the meal was finished Hauck and Birds Landing, together with Rascombe, took their departure to join the Indian where he had set up camp. The four of them sat late into the night around the fire. The weather had turned and it was cold. A wind was blowing off the mountains; the sky was overcast and snow was in the offing. It would be falling in the higher ranges.

'Gonna be bad in the hills,' Rascombe commented.

'Gonna be bad for Dement,' Hauck said.

'How you figure to find him?'

'Leave that to Birds Landing. She can track a gopher to its hole. She knows these mountains better'n anybody.'

'Seems like Dement is likely to be lookin' for you. You got those stamps.'

'That's what I figure. Someone representin' Dement is likely to make contact.'

'Maybe Dement himself?'

Hauck shook his head. 'I doubt it,' he replied. 'He'll be keepin' to the security of his lair same as I gather he always does. Nope, whatever happens down here in Pine Hollow, I figure we're goin' to have to go searchin' for the main man.'

★ ★ ★

A couple of days later they saw off Eustacia on the eastbound train, accompanied by Edwina. Hauck and Otoktay rode alongside the train for a short distance while Eustacia leaned out of the window and waved. At last they drew up and watched as her fluttering handkerchief faded from sight.

'Magaskawee will be safe now,' the

old Indian said. 'She has good medicine.'

Hauck thought of the parfleche Birds Landing had given him all those years ago. It had certainly proved effective. As they rode back to camp a sleety rain began to fall.

'The quicker we get movin' now the better,' Hauck said. 'It's goin' to be hard enough gettin' up to wherever Dement is hidin' out.'

They had been preparing for the ride, buying in clothing, equipment and arms. They were just about ready. Hauck decided to give it the rest of the day to see if Dement would make an approach. He felt confident that Dement would be aware of their arrival in Pine Hollow. The girl was of no use to him now. It was the stamps he was after and Hauck had them. Robbins would have had his instructions. After they had eaten he got to his feet and walked over to the appaloosa.

'You stay here,' he said to Rascombe and Hobbs, 'in case Dement tries to make contact. Me an' Birds Landing will ride into town, see if we can flush anybody out.'

They climbed into leather and rode away. Birds Landing had some things still to buy and made her way to the general store. Hauck was feeling thirsty and went to the Blue Nugget saloon. He stood at the bar and ordered whiskey. It was late afternoon but already the saloon was busy. A group of cowboys at one table were playing faro. In the corner a piano tinkled. Several men stood at the bar alongside Hauck. Presently one moved up alongside him. Hauck looked at him in the bar mirror. He was thin and grizzled. Hauck also took notice of the two other men along the bar he had been drinking with. The stranger slung back a slug of whiskey and then reached for Hauck's bottle.

'Hope you don't mind,' he said.

Hauck shrugged. 'Help yourself. Looks like you need it.'

The man stared at him. 'What do you mean by that?' he said.

'Take it whatever way you want.'

The man hesitated, seeming to make an effort to control himself before pouring a stiff drink. Hauck observed as his gaze swung towards the others standing at the end of the bar. The man finished his drink and reached for the bottle when Hauck's hand fell on his arm.

'One drink,' he said. 'You've had it.'

The man was about to react when one of the other two spoke. 'OK, Arlo,' he said. 'Take it easy.' He turned to Hauck. 'He gets a bit edgy when he's had a drink. Fact is, we ride for Mr Dement. Mr Dement thinks you have somethin' for him. In view of everythin' that's happened an' all, he thinks you might fail to make a delivery.'

Hauck remained silent.

'That's what we're doin' here. So if you just hand over that envelope you've got in your pocket, everythin' will be fine.'

Hauck moved slightly away from the bar. 'Maybe I'd better deliver it personally to Mr Dement,' he said.

The man gave him a sneering look. He glanced towards the others.

'Can't see no harm in that,' he said. 'But first I'd like to see the merchandise.'

Hauck paused for a moment. 'Yeah,' he said. 'Why not?' He reached into his pocket where he had put the envelope. It wasn't there. He felt inside another pocket, although he knew it wasn't in that one. He hadn't thought about the stamps since they had left Prairie Junction. There was no time to think about them now.

'Seems like I left 'em behind,' he said.

The man's face turned ugly. 'Hand over the goods,' he replied. 'No foolin' around.'

'Like to oblige but, as I said, I ain't got them with me right now.'

'I don't believe you. You're lyin'.'

The piano player ceased playing. Hauck tossed back the whiskey. The men beside him began to edge slowly away from the bar and the bartender, wiping a wet glass with a towel, made a gesture towards the shelf under the bar where Hauck knew he had a shotgun. Almost imperceptibly Hauck moved his head and the barman walked very slowly towards the end of the bar. In the mirror Hauck could see the faro players look up and begin to move back their chairs. He could see the two gunmen along the bar from him. He knew they were gunmen because they wore *buscadero* gunbelts with the guns low and tied with thongs. They were unshaven and looked mean. The one addressed as Arlo had moved back alongside them.

'Looks like he ain't denyin' it,' one of them said. The others began to laugh.

'I say you're a dirty, low-down, stinkin' prairie dog,' Arlo said.

Hauck slowly reached for the whiskey glass on the bar counter. He stretched out a hand and poured himself another drink from the bottle the bartender had placed there.

'Maybe he don't hear too well,' one of the gunmen remarked.

'Maybe he's a coward as well as a liar.'

Hauck lifted the glass to his lips, taking time to assess the position of the gunmen. The one who had been doing most of the talking was in the centre of the group. The other two had been standing one on each side but as Hauck watched they were already beginning to fan out. Two of them held their hands hovering close to the handles of their guns. The other wore a single gun holstered with its butt foremost. He also wore it on the left hip which meant making a cross draw. His arm would have further to carry.

Hauck had his plan. He would fire at the loudmouth first, then the one fingering his revolver. He would hit the floor and take the other, hoping he was right about the cross draw. Tilting the glass back, he swallowed the whiskey and turned to face the trio.

'So you ain't deaf after all,' the

gunslinger quipped.

Hauck looked closely at him. He was about thirty, so he probably had experience of these situations. He had survived, which signified he was an efficient killer. Hauck was keenly aware of the situation: the drop of sweat on his opponent's brow and the slight movements of the other two men. He watched the gunman's eyes, knowing that a slight alteration of the direction of his gaze might signify the moment he would go for his gun.

'I seen that pinto hitched outside too.'

Hauck said nothing.

'That's an Injun hoss.'

The man was beginning to run out of things to say. Hauck noticed the slight flicker of his eyes and even as the man's hand dropped to the handle of his gun Hauck's Colt was spitting lead. Two shots hit the gunman in the chest and shoulder and blasted him backwards. In almost the same instant Hauck turned and fired at the second gunman. The shot took him in the throat as the man's own gun fired harmlessly into the ceiling. Down he went, blood pouring in pulsing spurts from his wound.

Without hesitation Hauck flung himself forward as the third gunslick's shot rang out, creasing his brow. As soon as he hit the ground he rolled and, steadying himself for a fraction of a second, he loosed a fourth and fifth shot. The fourth shot took the man in the belly, the fifth in the chest and, because Hauck was firing from below, exited from the left shoulder and went ricocheting round the saloon.

For a few moments the man remained standing, an expression of bewilderment on his features. Then his legs sagged under him and he sank to his knees before falling forward, his head crashing against the side of the saloon bar.

Hauck did not stop to observe any of this. He was on his feet and bending over the outlaw who had been shot in the throat. Blood was pouring from his mouth and he was making a choking, gurgling sound as he attempted to speak. Then his head sank back and he was dead.

The saloon was silent, a silence which seemed almost palpable after the thunderous noise of the guns. Smoke billowed through the air and the atmosphere was heavy with the smell of cordite. Things seemed frozen in a moment of time. There was shock and disbelief on the faces of the barman and some of his customers. The action of the whole incident had been so swift.

Then the piano tinkled as the piano player nervously ran his fingers over the keys. It was like a signal for normality to be resumed. The faro players moved their seats back to the table. People began to talk and the barman's head appeared above the corner of the bar where he had taken refuge.

'Guess somebody had better fetch the undertaker,' Hauck said. He flung some coins on the bar. 'That should pay for any damage,' he said. 'I guess the marshal will be across soon. Tell him he can contact me at the general store.'

Taking one last look about him, Hauck walked slowly to the batwings and out into the street. Apart from a slight hubbub behind him, everything was normal. Further down the board-walk Birds Landing emerged from the general store, carrying a parcel. She started walking towards him, smiling as she approached.

'Get what you wanted?' Hauck said. She nodded. 'Good. Guess we can head back now. But we'll need to make a call at the marshal's office on the way.'

Birds Landing gave him a puzzled look.

'Dement's boys made contact,' he said. 'Afraid I had to disappoint them.'

6

The day following the incident in the Blue Nugget, Hauck, Birds Landing, Rascombe, Hobbs and Otoktay rode off into the hills. Apart from everything else, Hauck had a more personal reason now for seeking out Dement; the graze along his brow was a reminder of how close he had come to taking up residence in Boot Hill. The old Indian seemed even keener to catch up with Dement. Hauck might have been wrong, maybe it was the wind, but he thought he had detected a watery glint in Otoktay's eye as he waved goodbye to Eustacia.

The weather had truly broken; it was raining heavily as they left Pine Hollow and by the afternoon it had turned to snow. A cold wind blew down from the peaks and they were grateful for the heavy sheepskin coats and leather gloves they had purchased.

They camped that evening in the shelter of some rocks but before dawn they were on the trail again, climbing higher into the Blue Smoke ranges. The snow had lessened but still swirled about in the blustery gusts of wind. The path began to climb more steeply. It was slippery and the horses' hoofs sank into mud. Patches of snow lay across the path, and in the woods on either side it was lying thick and had drifted against the pale trunks of trees. The wind whistled in the pines.

They were riding single file with Hauck in the lead. As they reached the crest of the slope he glanced back at the others coming up behind him. The topmost peaks were beginning to glow with the first gleams of the rising sun. Overhead a few stars still glimmered. With a gentle touch of his knees he turned the appaloosa.

After a time the trail broadened out a little. On his right the land sloped away, clothed with stands of pine and aspen, and on the opposite side swelled upwards to the dim skyline. Waterfalls ran down the flanks of the mountain and the riders splashed through streams flowing across the track. They were headed north and west, travelling slowly.

It seemed to be getting colder. The higher ridges and summits, briefly revealed, were beginning to vanish again in low grey clouds. Hauck reckoned it was time to take a rest and he wanted to consult with Otoktay and Birds Landing. As they came round a bend in the trail he saw a small basin with groves of aspen which would provide shelter. He pulled up and turned in the saddle.

'We'll take a break!' he shouted.

He rode into the hollow and swung down, his saddle creaking. He moved to where Birds Landing had pulled up, to offer her his hand, but with a lithe movement she had already dismounted. He looked in her eyes. There was no sign of tiredness or discomfort. They looked eagerly back into his own and he realized she was enjoying this as much as he was. She looked eager and excited. He realized too that although she might look frail she was as tough as they came.

They mounted up again and set off along the trail. The country was getting wilder and more rugged and the horses were not finding it easy going. Hauck was on the alert. It was very unlikely that they would be spotted by any of Dement's men, but he kept a close lookout. He realized that perhaps their best weapon was the element of surprise and he did not want to lose it.

'We leave the trail soon,' Birds Landing said.

They rode on a little further till they reached a point where there was evidence of rock falls. She led the way into the thinning trees. It was darker and any landmarks soon disappeared but she seemed able to find her way. Hauck followed immediately behind her, the rest continuing to follow in single file. The trees stood in rows and there was a surprising amount of space. The horses' hoofs made no sound as they trod the needle-strewn floor. Snow hung from the boughs of trees and had drifted in places but it was patchy.

Soon the forest began to thin and they emerged on to a slope below some caves. They came round a side of the mountain and suddenly the ground fell away before them to reveal a magnificent panorama of lofty snow-capped peaks, sweeping valleys and canyons. Birds Landing stopped and Hauck came alongside her.

'We go down,' she said pointing. 'After that I'm not so certain.'

In front of them a broad shelf sloped gradually before rising again to form a ridge, while behind them the great shoulder of the mountain they had just ridden up jutted out, forming a natural barrier. The other riders came alongside.

'Sure is one hell of a view,' Hobbs remarked.

'Who knows, there could be gold in those ranges.'

They sat their horses to admire the scene.

'Let's move,' Hauck said eventually.

They started down the slope. Snow was lying more deeply on this side and the wind was blowing strong. They moved carefully until they reached the bottom and began the long climb to the ridge. The short daylight hours were fading towards the west and already shadows were creeping down from the mountain heights. The higher peaks which had been so gloriously revealed were hidden now behind banks of cloud.

After reaching the top of the rise they crossed a windswept plateau before the contours of the land led them down through another stand of trees. They began to look around for somewhere to camp for the night. Hearing the sound of running water and locating its source among some rocks and aspen trees a short distance from the trail they were following, Hauck pulled up.

'Reckon this will do as good as anywheres!' he called to the others.

Although in simple terms of distance they had not ridden that far, both men and horses were tired and ready to call it a day. It had been hard, laborious riding and despite their sheepskin coats and slickers they were cold. The place offered shelter from the wind. Soon they had a fire going. They rubbed the horses down with evergreen needles and fed them and then set about feeding themselves. They were well prepared, anticipating that it might take some time to locate their target.

By the time night had come they had made themselves tolerably comfortable and were feeling fairly satisfied with their progress. The next day might be more difficult.

Before morning came they were on their way. A slight thaw had set in. Ahead of them the mountain wall seemed to offer no break and for the first time Hauck began to question whether they were on the right track. His doubts were soon laid to rest. Coming up behind him, Birds Landing pointed to something to the side of the trail.

'Stop!' she said.

Dropping from the leather, she walked over. Hauck dismounted and joined her.

'Old horse droppings,' she said. 'Maybe three, four days.'

Hauck nodded and grinned. 'Looks like we're on the right trail,' he said.

They mounted up and moved on. Hauck took out his field glasses and took a close look at the escarpment. He couldn't be certain, but he thought he detected what might be an opening in the cliff face. He handed the glasses to Otoktay.

'Could be a keyhole pass. I think it's a gap. I guess we got no choice.'

Hauck was thinking. If it was a gap it might be a box canyon. There were probably many of them leading nowhere. On the other hand, if it did lead somewhere, it would be an ideal place to defend. He put himself in the position of Dement and his gunslicks. If they were holed up somewhere this would be the ideal back door. He raised the glasses and scanned the slopes. They were steep, too steep for a man to climb. Yet somehow he felt exposed and his hand instinctively reached towards the Winchester in its scabbard.

They were closer now and could see that there was clearly an opening in the cliff face. The reason it had remained hidden was that it led into the mountain at an angle. The slope before it was covered in snow and bringing their horses up was not an easy manoeuvre. The entrance was narrow and dark and led upward quite steeply. Hauck considered for a moment, then, dismounting, took the reins and led his horse till the ground levelled out and he swung back into the saddle. The others followed his example and came up behind him in an uneven line.

The pass was little more than a gash in the side of the mountain and the rock walls loomed high overhead, cutting out the light. The horses did not like it; their ears were pricked and they shied at obstacles along the narrow path. Hauck was keenly aware of how vulnerable they were to attack. It would be difficult even to turn the horses.

He kept looking up at the towering rock faces on either side, but it seemed they offered no possibility of concealment. They were inaccessible and the only risk was that there might be some sort of trail across the summit, but it seemed unlikely.

One thing working in their favour was that the rock walls were too steep to allow snow to accumulate. It clung to the sides of the mountain in patches where there were outcrops or indentations. If the walls had been less steep and snow had gathered there might have been a danger of falls, especially with the temporary thaw.

The trail took a turn and Hauck was

met with a blast of wind whistling down the canyon. He huddled deeper into his sheepskin coat. Behind him came the sound of the horses' hoofs and the creaking of leather. It was an eerie place.

After a further couple of miles his ears picked up another sound and he looked up to see water falling like tears down the mountainside with ferns and a few bushes growing alongside. Water flowed over the trail and the horses splashed through. For some time the trail had been leading downhill and it was with a sense of relief that Hauck observed that it was beginning to widen. He had been growing more and more concerned that it might not lead anywhere.

Gradually the high granite walls began to draw back and the shadows on the trail started to lift. Then the trail broadened further and descended more steeply and Hauck could see that they were emerging into a high mountain valley. It lay below them like a dish streaked with snow and ice and surrounded on all sides by the towering walls of the mountains. He reined in his horse and signalled to the others to do likewise.

'I got a feelin',' he said.

'Me too,' Otoktay confirmed.

Leaving the others to watch the horses, the two of them moved forward on foot to reconnoitre. There was plenty of cover in the form of rocks and boulders as they worked their way forward to a rim which overlooked the valley.

'Looks like we found it,' Hauck said.

Below them on the valley floor under the shelter of a high snowy peak was a large, rambling ranch-style house with some scattered buildings behind which a number of horses were corralled. Smoke rose in a thin feather from the ranch house and they could see some figures moving between the buildings. Hauck surveyed the scene through his field glasses before passing them to Otoktay.

'What I don't understand,' he said, 'is why they don't have guards posted somewhere along the pass.'

'Why should they expect any visitors?'

'Maybe you're right,' Hauck said. 'But we'd better be careful now.'

They made their way back to the others and reported what they had seen. The men exchanged glances.

'OK,' Hauck said. 'I don't know about the rest of you, but I could do with some food inside of me.'

They led their horses back down the canyon a little way till they found a suitable spot among the rocks.

'When we move, we'll leave the horses here,' Hauck said.

They tended to the horses, then sat among the rocks to eat cold pemmican washed down with water, since lighting a fire was out of the question. As they ate Hauck looked up at the mountainside. Sections of jagged rock and scree indicated where there had been rock falls in the past which accounted for the debris on the canyon floor. He wondered again if there was any route up there on the mountain top. His thoughts were interrupted by a question from Rascombe.

'How long do you aim to sit here?' he asked.

'Just as long as it takes,' Hauck replied.

He sensed the tension that had arisen now that Dement's stronghold had been reached.

'Why don't we just ride right on down?' Hobbs asked.

'That's one option,' Hauck replied. 'It might well work, but there'd be no way we'd all come out alive. There are other ways.'

'If we could surround the place without being observed, we'd have them cold,' Otoktay said.

'That's the way I figure it,' Hauck replied. 'Apart from that high peak directly above the ranch, the valley slopes pretty gently till just above the timber line. I figure if we can get into the shelter of those trees we could more or less have them covered.'

He paused. 'If we succeed, once the firing starts some of the varmints are likely to head for the pass. There may be other ways in and out of the valley — probably are, because they seem to move about with relative ease — but if they do decide to head this way it might be a good idea to leave someone here to block them off.'

He turned to Birds Landing. 'How about if you remain here and take on that job? You can keep an eye on the horses too.'

While they finished eating Hauck and Otoktay arranged their dispositions. Hauck wished there were more of them.

'Don't anyone shoot till the signal's given,' Hauck said.

'What'll that be?'

'Leave it to me. I ain't spent time in the mountains without hearing a wolf howl. Reckon I can do a real good imitation.' He looked around at the others clutching their rifles. 'Everyone knows what to do?' he asked.

The men nodded in confirmation. 'Sure. Let's go get the varmints.'

They moved forward to the point at which Hauck and Otoktay had surveyed the valley and Hauck pointed out certain features of the land and where approximately he wanted everyone to be. They commenced to move out, clambering over the rocky mountainside and keeping to whatever cover the mountain provided till they reached the cover of the trees. They were led by Hauck and Otoktay, who were taking positions at the furthest points almost underneath the tall mountain which reared its snowy peak high above the scene. By opting for these vantage points, Hauck figured it would give the others plenty of time to get into position so they should be ready when he took up his own.

Crouched low, he moved between the trees. Snow lay on the ground and had drifted deep in places. A cold wind blew through the pines threatening further falls. At times Hauck caught glimpses of the buildings below but he didn't stop to take in further details. The trees were thin here and the going was becoming very difficult. The slope of the mountain was steeper and he was hampered by drifts of snow.

He slipped behind a low outcrop of rock and kneeled down. He took his guns from their holsters and checked that they were ready for action. Then he checked his rifle. Lying flat, he surveyed the scene below.

The camp appeared to have become quite animated. Numbers of men were walking about and some were sitting on the corral fence while another was leading a horse on a rope. Although he strained his ears to listen for sounds, Hauck could hear nothing. The wind was blowing and clouds were billowing in from the north but the sky overhead was fairly clear. The sun broke through and a widening ray lit up the valley and fell in a roseate glow on the snowy high peaks.

The seconds and then the minutes ticked away. Momentarily Hauck was distracted by a gleam of sunlight flashing off something below, then he saw a wisp of smoke, which was followed immediately by the reverberation of a rifle shot. Before he had fully registered what had happened other shots rang out and he could see Dement's men begin to run towards the main building. Three of them were couched behind a barn pointing their rifles towards the mountain slopes. He realized that somehow they had been detected.

Immediately giving the wolf's-howl signal his finger slowly squeezed the trigger of the rifle and he returned fire. Instantly the mountainside blazed into activity as shots rang out from all around. He saw two of the running figures fling up their arms and fall to the ground but the rest seemed to have made it to the ranch house. Smoke was pouring from all the buildings as Dement's gunslicks returned fire and Hauck felt a movement in the air as a slug tore overhead and went whining away among the rocks. The horses were plunging and rearing down in the corral. His rifle was empty and he jerked more bullets into the chamber before opening fire again, aiming at the puffs of smoke which were coming from the windows of the buildings. The roar of gunfire was unabated but it was impossible to tell what was happening.

Hauck lay back and looked about him. The sun had retreated now behind the clouds and a thin rain began to drift down the valley. That meant more snow higher up. Above him the mountain soared into the heavens, its sheer sides scarred by landslides. A few gnarled and stunted trees clung to cracks in the rock, struggling to survive higher up the mountain. Leaning forward, Hauck could see rocks lying close to the nearer cabins.

As he was taking this all in, there

came a sudden fusillade of shots from the cabin. Then, from one of the barns, a group of riders emerged, riding hard and bending low over their saddles. Hauck's rifle was instantly in his hands, his finger squeezing the trigger. The Winchester belched flame and one of the horses went down. In the same instant one of the riders fell backwards and, his foot caught in the stirrup, was dragged along behind the galloping horse.

There were three riders left and they were heading up the trail towards the pass. Shots rang from the mountainside to his left and he saw another horse stagger, almost unseating its rider, before plunging on. Hauck had no more time to dwell on the matter because another group of men had burst from the main building and were heading for the corral, firing as they went. They obviously had no intention of getting trapped down there. Hauck thought they meant to reach the corral but they disappeared from view around the corner of a building from which they began to fire, taking aim at the stabs of flame and smoke issuing from the slopes above them.

Hauck decided he needed to get closer. Above him he could see smoke billowing from the trees where Otoktay was hidden. Calling to him for cover, he got to his feet and began to run down the slope. Bullets whined overhead and smacked into the hillside, but he managed to reach a clump of bushes without being hit. He began to edge his way around so that he could get an angle on the outlaws hiding around the side of the barn. He lay flat and crawled forward, hoping that the Indian's fire would keep them pinned down long enough till he reached the position he required.

The hillsides reverberated with the concentrated fire of Rascombe and Hobbs. He had no idea how many of Dement's men remained in the buildings or how many were wounded. What he wanted to avoid was more of them getting away as the other riders had done. He couldn't help thinking of Birds Landing. She was a good shot and there were only three of them left. She should be able to deal with them but he wished he had taken more measures to safeguard the pass. Slithering forwards he reached the rock shelter he had been making for and cautiously raised his head.

He had a good view of the corner of the barn where the outlaws were sheltering, and he began firing. He saw two of them go down. Another one spun round as a bullet took him in the shoulder, then he turned to run with the rest of them. They did not reappear and Hauck assumed they had entered the barn. He was about to reload when a shot came singing over his head, not from below but from a position above him.

He rolled over and saw a couple of gunslicks on the mountainside. Somehow they had got away from the camp and outflanked him. Quickly raising his rife he fired and as the smoke cleared a man came tumbling down the rocky slope. There was a burst of fire from Otoktay's direction and the other man doubled over screaming. Hauck could not tell how badly hurt he was. He lay still in case the man was in a position to fire further but there was only stillness. For a moment the sounds of shooting died down with only a few sporadic shots breaking the eerie silence.

Suddenly Hauck heard a new sound, a sound he couldn't place but which sounded like the passage of a distant train. At first faint, it began to grow in volume. He looked about, confused and at a loss to know what was happening. He thought it might be the wind rising, but no wind he had heard sounded quite like that. He felt a surge of panic such as he had never felt before as the noise grew to a thunder and rocks began to bounce about the mountain-side all around him.

In an instant the truth dawned and as he crouched for shelter he heard himself shouting 'Avalanche!' as if to warn anyone, as if anyone could possibly hear. He was overwhelmed by a feeling of complete and utter helplessness. There was nothing he could do but pray. The whole mountain seemed to be swaying and with an almighty roar a torrent of snow came rolling and sliding down the mountain-side, ripping up anything in its path and pushing great boulders and trees before it like children's toys. The noise was deafening.

Above the cascading snows hung huge clouds of silvery-white powder. Hauck saw the great white wall come hurtling towards him, then he was overwhelmed by the deadly weight of snow. The uproar and turmoil completely disoriented him but he had just enough presence of mind to roll himself into a ball and crouch as low as possible behind the flimsy shelter of the rock. He felt the snow piling up on top of him. It was jammed into his mouth, ears and nostrils and he could scarcely breathe. He could see nothing now. He was helpless and trapped and struggling to breathe. Then everything went black.

When he awakened he did not know what had happened or where he was. One arm was pinned beneath him but he could move the other. Reaching up into the blackness his fingers touched the roof only inches above his head. He was close to being seized by a blind panic. His first thought was that he had been buried alive, then he began to recall what had happened. The truth was hardly less bad. In effect he had indeed been buried alive. His head ached and there was a ringing in his ears.

Above him there was a narrow tunnel where his rifle had wedged against the rock. Trying as best he could to remain calm, he tried to move his body but it was no good. The snow was tight around him and he had no idea of how deep it might be. Where he had been crouching the rocks had served to create a pocket of air. Maybe air was getting to him somehow from outside.

He did not know how long it might be expected to last. So far as he could tell he was not badly injured. Apart from his aching head he felt no other pain. His main fear was of suffocation and then of cold. How much time before he froze to death? Fear was clouding his brain but he attempted to think logically.

He could not tell which direction was up and which was down, but he had no choice in the matter. Scope for any sort of action was severely limited. The only thing he could do was to try and push his free arm through the snow and hope that it might penetrate the surface. He raised it again and began to prod at the roof of snow. He pushed as hard as he could but the snow was packed tight and was unyielding. The tactics did not seem to be getting him anywhere and he needed to conserve oxygen. There didn't seem to be much else he could do.

His only hope lay in the prospect of

someone finding him. Otoktay had seen where he was on the mountainside, but had he survived the avalanche? The others were probably safe, but it depended on over how wide a front the collapse had occurred.

His thoughts ran on and became confused. He was worrying about Birds Landing and then he seemed to see her face. He instinctively reached for the charm she had given him and realized again that he was trapped. He was dreaming about the mountains, the high lonesome, and he was looking over a great open valley towards distant cloud-capped peaks and ridges where eagles swooped. The wind blew cleanly about him and the snow on the ranges was like a benediction. It made a soughing sound in the treetops and the leaves rattled. The rattling grew louder, then he came to full consciousness and realized that the sound was close at hand and that it was not the wind. The pitch darkness was suddenly stabbed by a blessed ray of light and a voice was calling to him.

'Cetanwakuwa, are you alive down there?'

He tried to speak but couldn't. The gap grew wider and an arm reached into his tomb.

'It's OK,' the voice said. 'Hang on. We'll soon have you out of it.' A face appeared — Otoktay's. So the Indian had found him after all. He was digging down with his hands and using his broad-bladed knife to chip away at the hard, impacted snow. It was slow going but eventually Hauck was able to move and with a voice he scarcely recognized he managed to acknowledge Otoktay's words.

He became aware that someone else was digging alongside Otoktay. He moved his arm again and then his body and at last, with a heave, he was free. Between them Otoktay and Hobbs lifted him out into the open. The sky was grey and snow was falling but the light still blinded him. There were tears running down his face. He had been restored to life again.

After a time he was able to look around him and take in what had happened. The mountain had changed. Where there had been rock and trees there was now just a huge blanket of snow. Embedded in it were boulders and trunks of trees. When he looked down to where the outlaw roost had been there was nothing to be seen but more snow piled high. The place was a blank, featureless desolation. The entire camp was buried deep. The buildings had disappeared; only the high roof of one of the barns emerged from its shroud of white.

'Better get down there,' Hauck said, thinking with a shudder of his terrible experience. The men buried beneath the tons of snow were the scourings of the earth but he would not have wished them a fate like that.

'Sure,' Hobbs said, 'but they wouldn't have had a chance.'

Suddenly Hauck remembered Birds

Landing and concern for the fate of the outlaws was driven from his mind.

'Birds Landing,' he said. 'Is she safe?'

Otoktay looked at him. Concern was suddenly etched on his face too. 'She knows how to look after herself,' he said.

'Some of those varmints broke loose,' Hauck said, 'before the avalanche. They were headed for the pass.'

Rascombe looked at Hauck. 'Yeah. I saw them too. And I reckon I recognized Dement. He was one of them.'

Without waiting any longer, Hauck and the others began to try to make their way across the slope. It was difficult. The snow sucked at their feet and they had to be careful to avoid deep drifts. At one point one of the men sank up to his armpits and had to be pulled out again. Hauck was afraid of starting another slippage.

High above them they could hear the mountain creaking. Hauck assumed that it was the firing which had triggered off the avalanche. The sun was low in the sky and snow was falling. They needed to get back to where they had left the horses, and not just for the sake of Birds Landing. Slowly and laboriously they continued along the side of the mountain. Hauck was beginning to feel the after-effects of his ordeal. He felt chilled to the bone and his head still ached. His chest and shoulders felt sore from the compression of the snow.

A strange dismal silence had descended over the valley, broken only by the wind which blew up curtains of fine snow as it whipped across the barren landscape. It seemed they would never reach their destination and the distance that had been so short earlier in the day, when they were taking their places in preparation for attacking the ranch, seemed to go on and on. They were all weary and it took a real effort and concentration to make their way through the snow. Eventually the going began to get easier as they neared the outer limits of the avalanche, and soon they were approaching the rise which led up to the entrance to the canyon.

Hauck seemed to gather strength from somewhere and pushed on ahead with Otoktay. Neither of them said anything but they were both feeling anxious. A cold hand was clutched around Hauck's heart. Something was wrong. Birds Landing should have come out to meet them. Then his eyes saw something lying in the snow on the side of the hill. He gasped and ran forward, fearing it was Birds Landing. As he approached he saw it was not her but one of Dement's gunslicks. His head had been shot away and he must have died instantly. There was no trace of Birds Landing. Some of the other men had joined them and they began to look around for her, fearing what they might find.

'Ealaothek-kaunis!' Hauck called, using her Indian name. The others added their voices, shouting for Birds Landing and using her English name of Julia, but it was to no avail. Birds Landing was gone.

When they had finally given up the search Hauck felt almost relieved, but then, with the full realization of what must have happened to her, he was sunk into a deep gloom. There was evidence of the movement of several horses. Two of their own horses were missing. It was fairly apparent that the three outlaws had ridden up here and then taken Birds Landing with them, taking one horse for her and the other to replace the wounded horse which Hauck had seen stagger. Of that horse there was no sign. Hauck reckoned it must have followed the others down the canyon. He looked for signs of blood but there wasn't any. If the outlaw's horse had been hit by a slug it must only have grazed it.

Night was coming down and they had to admit defeat. Some of the men were for moving straight on but both Hauck and Otoktay knew it was no good. Quite apart from the dangers of riding such an unknown trail in the dark, they would be unable to find sign either within the canyon or beyond. The men were exhausted. Anxious as they all were to do something, the sensible thing was to make camp for the night, get some rest, and then resume the trail at first light.

They were in a position now to assess their own casualties and only Rascombe had sustained a minor wound. Hauck realized that they had been lucky. There would have been more casualties had not the avalanche put an end to hostilities. Their good fortune also owed something to his tactics. All in all it would have been a very satisfactory outcome if it were not for what had happened in the pass. That put a downer on everything.

Hauck cursed himself for leaving Birds Landing at the entrance to the pass. He had thought she would be comparatively safe there, but things had turned out differently. As they sat by the fire he watched Otoktay in the flickering light. The Indian rose to his feet and walked across to where his friend was sitting slightly apart from the rest.

'I'm sorry,' he said.

'It ain't your fault,' Hauck replied. 'I shouldn't have left her here.'

Otoktay uttered a strained laugh. 'I'd like to have seen you try and stop her,' he replied.

They were both silent after that. Snow was falling through the night sky and it was as cold as the splinter in Hauck's soul.

'Like I say, she can take care of herself,' Otoktay said after some time.

Hauck knew it was true but the reflection brought neither of them any consolation.

'Get some sleep,' Otoktay said. 'You need it.'

Hauck nodded. 'At first light we ride,' he said, 'and we won't stop till we find Birds Landing.'

7

It took a long time but eventually Hauck slept. It was a troubled sleep which brought unwanted dreams. When he awoke it was dark but Otoktay was already up and about. He had a fire going and bacon sizzling in a pan.

'No point in goin' hungry,' he said.

Hauck agreed with his sentiments but found he could not eat anything. Instead he downed several cups of hot black coffee before taking Rascombe and Hobbs along with him to see to the horses. Snow had continued to fall during the night and they cleared a space so the horses could graze. Hauck was anxious now to get started and so were the others. Long before sunup they had entered the dark recesses of the canyon, riding single file just as they had done coming the opposite way.

Snow was falling more heavily now. It

seemed that the thaw was over. A biting wind swirled around the high canyon walls and there was ice on the path. Hauck, anxious to get through the narrow canyon before there was any possibility they might be blocked in, was on the lookout for any repetition of what had happened the day before. It seemed to him that there was a lot more snow on the mountainsides and some of it looked pretty precarious. He had been through a bad scare and each time he looked up he felt uneasy. It seemed like it didn't take much to bring it down. Although each one of them was keen to get through the canyon they rode at a slow and even pace. They were going uphill and the trail was becoming particularly narrow.

Coming round a slight bend Hauck drew up suddenly, holding up his hand for the others to do likewise. Ahead of them the narrow trail was blocked by a landslide. Hauck slid from the leather and walked up to it. Across the trail and standing about four feet high was a wall of rock. Looking at it more closely and seeing how some of the rocks fitted together, Hauck was convinced that it was not accidental. He looked up at the sides of the canyon. They seemed sheer but maybe there was scope for a climber to get part of the way up. Below a slight indentation, the sides of the mountain were scarred. Some larger boulders still remained above the indentation and hanging over it were a few dwarf bristle-cone pines. Hauck went to examine the wall of the canyon beside the trail. Sure enough the surface of the rock was marked where a boot had scuffed over it. Otoktay joined him.

'You think it's deliberate?' Hauck asked him.

'Yes,' Otoktay replied. 'It seems they were expecting us.'

Hauck's gaze surveyed the high rock walls. 'No place for a gunman to be concealed,' he said. 'They just wanted to slow us down.'

'They didn't do a great job of it.

Maybe they were worried about time, or maybe there just weren't enough rocks.'

Without more ado they set about dragging aside the obstruction. It wasted more time in clearing a path through than Hauck had anticipated, but it was more of a nuisance than a serious setback. When they had finished they remounted and stepped their horses through the gap. Hauck was more careful than ever now to keep watch on the mountainsides, just in case there could be an ambush.

It was a nervy ride. The sun had risen but the canyon remained in shadow. Snow continued to fall. After what seemed an eternity they at last approached the steep downhill slope to the canyon mouth and Hauck dismounted to lead his horse down the slippery treacherous track. The others followed his example and soon they emerged on to the slope beyond. Standing forlornly some way off with its head down was the horse the outlaws had exchanged. Hauck's surmise was correct. Slightly injured, it had followed the outlaws through the pass. Hobbs rode out to retrieve it. Hauck swung down from the appaloosa and examined the ground.

'Horses,' he said. 'What do you think, Otoktay?'

In the lee of the rock wall the ground was churned. Snow had partly drifted over it but the Sioux's practised eye told him there had been riders and probably more than had come through the pass.

'Looks to me like there were riders coming in from this direction and they joined the ones coming through the canyon.'

'More outlaws?'

'I guess so. Probably a few stragglers returning to the roost. Likely they met up with the others and set off along the side of the mountain.'

'How many of 'em?'

'Can't tell. Maybe three or four.'

Hauck was thinking. They were all tired and Rascombe was carrying a gunshot wound in the upper arm. They had done what they set out to do. Dement and his remaining gunmen had a good start on them but not so good that they couldn't be caught. It wouldn't be easy tracking them and the pursuers would need to move swiftly. He didn't like to think of what Dement might do to Birds Landing. Once he thought through the options open to them his mind was made up. Hobbs and Rascombe should return down the mountain while he and Otoktay would carry on the pursuit. When he put his proposal to the men there were some objections, but not from Otoktay.

'Hauck's right,' he said. 'Him and me can move quickly.'

In the end the others were persuaded. After loading provisions on to a packhorse Hauck and Otoktay rode off in one direction and Hobbs and Rascombe in the other.

'They done well,' Otoktay said.

For a long while they rode in silence, holding close to the mountainside. The trail would have been difficult to follow at any time, but now that it was blown over with snow it was virtually non-existent. The snow had ceased to fall but the biting wind was even more bitter. They were climbing steadily and were beginning to turn in a westerly direction, which would take them round the shoulder of the mountain. On their right the bench fell away but there was little they could see because of mist and cloud and a thin veil of sleety vapour. The ground became even steeper and they began to switchback their way up to try and preserve the strength of their horses.

At last, as darkness started to fall they stopped to camp beneath an overhang of rock. After they had eaten and built themselves a smoke, Otoktay voiced the question which had been in both their minds.

'Where do you think they could be heading?'

Hauck had no ready answer. 'Maybe they haven't thought it through,' he said. 'Maybe they're just running.'

'Or maybe there's a trail through in this direction that we don't know anything about,' Otoktay conjectured.

They turned in to snatch some sleep, but in the early hours Hauck awoke. It was very cold and the horses, which they had brought in close, were standing together with their heads down. There was a strange glow about the night; Hauck got up to investigate and saw that it was caused by ice gleaming in the light of a moon moving through scudding clouds. There was ice on the horses' coats and Hauck wiped it off before tossing some extra branches on the fire. He stood and looked out. It was a strangely beautiful and haunting scene, and very lonely. It was the top of the world, fierce and unforgiving. It answered to something in Hauck's own nature. He drank in the clear sharp air and felt empty, but he was glad to have Otoktay along.

The next morning they breakfasted

on coffee and sourdough bread before saddling up and moving out. It was a slow ride, the horses moving stiffly over the frozen ground, picking up their feet. Patches of cloud hung low over the mountains; flakes of snow drifted through air, but there was a promise of heavy snow to come. When it fell and lay over the ice the going would be even more dangerous and there would be a high risk of the horses breaking a leg. The packhorse was unhappy and pulling at the lead rope.

Suddenly Hauck's appaloosa, stepping off the trail, began to flounder in deep snow. Hauck hauled on the reins as the animal went plunging and snorting through the drift till it found its feet again on more solid ground.

'If it's bad for us,' Otoktay said, 'remember it's bad for them too.'

Hauck considered the situation. They were up in the tundra region with the tree line far below. The going was getting tougher and tougher and when the snow arrived it would be almost impossible for the horses to find a footing.

'I think we should leave the horses behind,' Hauck said.

Otoktay agreed and they started to unpack the items they would need, before clearing the snow and ice for a distance around to provide the horses with grass. They fed them and gave them a final rubdown. Then they slung their packs across their shoulders and walked away. The horses stood still with their heads bowed watching them.

'They have a better chance this way,' Otoktay said. 'They'll find their way back.'

Hauck had already forgotten them. He was concentrating his efforts on the climb and keeping his eyes open for any sign of the outlaws. The weather closed in and they had to battle against the driving snow. They found a recess in the rock wall in which to shelter while they ate a miserable meal of jerky washed down with water. Then they resumed walking till what little daylight there was began to fade away.

They were looking for a place to camp among some rocks when Hauck's keen eyes detected a glimmer of something near by. At first he thought nothing of it. Maybe it was just a piece of ice or some mica in the rock. Then he thought again and walked back to where he had seen it. Wedged into a crack of the rock where it was protected from the snow was a bead necklace similar to the one he had been given by Birds Landing.

'Look here!' he called.

Otoktay came scrambling over. Hauck held up the necklace.

'Birds Landing!' the Sioux exclaimed.

They exchanged glances. Their faces were covered, but each could see the glint in the other's eyes.

'They can't be far ahead of us. The snow is fresh.'

They looked about for further sign but the snow had covered everything other than the sheltered surfaces of the rocks. Had the gunmen discarded their horses too? Hauck was becoming convinced that they were heading for an unknown pass which would begin to lead them back down from the high country. He looked about but the view was obscured by driving snow. Filled with fresh hope, they determined to push on a little further before night fell, continuing as far as they were able on the same route as the one they had been following. They moved on but soon the pelting snow and the darkness combined to convince them they must shelter for the night.

By the time they had built a fire in the lee of the rocks and eaten they were feeling in better spirits. Conditions were bad but they were both hardened to them. Hauck had a feeling that if it wasn't for worrying about Birds Landing, they would both be relishing their current circumstances. It was like a throwback to old times. Hauck had built himself a smoke and after taking a deep pull he sat forward and reached for the coffee pot.

'Hell,' he said, 'I don't know about you, but I could do with some of this.' He poured coffee into his tin mug, then did the same for Otoktay, who held a finger to his mouth.

'Listen,' he said.

Hauck leaned his head slightly to one side. He could hear the crackling of the flames, the rushing of the wind and the underlying sibilant insistent falling of snow. He could hear his heart beating. He became aware of the mighty invisible peaks all around and the silence in which all things were enfolded.

'We'll both be fine when we've found Birds Landing,' he said.

'This is where I want to die,' Otoktay said, 'among the mountains, not down there in the towns among strangers. The mountains are not strangers. The creatures that live here are not strangers: the deer, the elk, the bears. Up here I feel the Wakan Tanka.'

'You ain't goin' to die for a long time yet,' Hauck replied.

'It don't matter when,' the Sioux said. 'Just so long as Birds Landing is safe.'

Hauck glanced at him. There was something ambiguous in the old Sioux warrior's words. Just then Otoktay raised his arm into the air.

'There!' he said. 'Listen again.'

Once more Hauck became conscious of the sounds of the night. Then, from somewhere a long ways distant, faint and haunting, he heard the long lonesome howl of a wolf.

Morning came. While it was still dark Hauck and Otoktay prepared to continue the search. As they were about to set out into the swirling snow Otoktay produced a bundle from his pack.

'What you got there?' Hauck said.

'Just something I brought along.'

He undid the bundle and produced two pairs of snowshoes. They were crudely made of long thin branches bent back to make a rough oval on to which strips of rawhide had been fastened to form a web.

'I figured there could be a use for them once we got into the high country.'

Otoktay took the lead and, considering the conditions, set a good pace. They were feeling confident now and did not notice the freezing cold wind as it bit at their faces. The snow continued to fall and there was little to be seen. They were moving across a bare plateau towards a ridge which rose steeply and formed a sharp serrated edge, now softened by the driving snow and cloud. Hauck had found the makeshift snowshoes awkward at first but now that he was getting accustomed to them he found that they helped to make the going easier.

After a time Otoktay halted. He knew it was important to conserve their strength, and the danger of working up a sweat. Then they moved on again. It was just hard slogging, putting out one foot after another. One thing in their favour was that as the snow iced over it became firm and provided a more solid footing. All the same, they needed to be careful to avoid any looser drifts. Hauck remembered how his horse had walked into one and how it had floundered.

As they approached the ridge the wind seemed to get stronger, howling along the line of the escarpment. There were rockfalls and boulders lying at the foot of the cliffs ahead of them and behind these was a cleft in the rock face.

They were now presented with a problem. Should they follow the line of the escarpment or should they enter the cleft, which might lead to a pass beyond? It was a lottery but everything depended on the answer. Otoktay had stopped and Hauck came up alongside him. Suddenly Hauck felt a sharp tear along the side of his head followed by an explosion; he couldn't tell if it was outside or inside his skull. Clutching his head he fell to the ground as something whined overhead and there was a succession of loud bangs which reverberated back from the cliff face. He realized they were under fire and he had been hit. Everything went black, but he came round again instantly to find Otoktay bending over him.

Ignoring the bullets which were singing all around, the Indian took Hauck in his arms and began to stagger through the snow in the direction from which they had come. His instinct was to run towards the rocks but he realized that that was where the shots were coming from, so instead he sought the comparative shelter of a snow-filled depression in the ground. He moved as quickly as he could but the snow hampered him and Hauck was a heavy burden.

About halfway to his destination he stumbled and went crashing to the ground. Bullets were still sending up plumes of snow around him and instinctively he flung himself on top of Hauck. He felt a pain in his left leg, then a bullet ricocheted from the pack he was carrying. Gritting his teeth against the pain, he rose to his feet, took up his burden and stumbled on.

The snowdrift was only yards away but the pain in his leg was intense and he could only move with agonising slowness, dragging his leg behind him. As another bullet whistled by him he reached the snowdrift and tumbled down behind it. He unloaded his rifle, then managed to turn over on his stomach and begin a rapid fire in the direction of the rocks.

He could not see anybody and was shooting blind. Hauck had lost consciousness again but came round and, realizing the situation, joined Otoktay, firing in the direction of the rocks. He was bleeding badly from a head wound and the blood was getting into his eyes. He jerked more cartridges into the magazine and started a new round of firing. Lead was being flung back at them but the tempo of gunfire began to diminish. A few more random shots rang out, then there was stillness, a stillness made all the more powerful by contrast with the uproar which had preceded it.

Hauck reached up to feel his head. The bleeding was heavy but it seemed the wound was not serious. Another half an inch and he would have been dead. As it was there was a nasty gash about three inches long where the bullet had creased the side of his head. When he turned to Otoktay he could see that the Indian's case was more serious. Otoktay's leg had been shattered below the knee and he had taken another bullet in the shoulder. Slowly Hauck raised himself up and looked towards the rocks. He could see nothing but the blinding snow. He realized that it was probably the snow that had saved them, blurring the gunmen's vision and providing a moving curtain to screen himself and Otoktay.

With that came another realization: that he owed his life to Otoktay. The Sioux had risked his own life to carry him from the snowfield where he would have presented an easy target, and again when he had lain on top of him to protect him from gunfire. It was then that Otoktay had been hit.

Hauck remained motionless till he was satisfied that the shooting was over. Then he turned to Otoktay. He was lying with his eyes closed but as Hauck approached they opened and a grin spread across his features.

'We know where they are now,' he said.

'Can you move?' Hauck asked. 'We need to get into cover.'

Otoktay shook his head. 'Leave me,' he said. 'You go and get them.'

Hauck did not reply. Instead he put the Indian's arm round his shoulder and with a huge effort hoisted him on to his back. Otoktay was quite a big man and it took all Hauck's strength to carry him, but he started out into the swirling snowstorm, heading for the rocks. He was taking a big risk. If the gunmen were still there he would be a target.

The snow was driving down and, obscuring the landscape, provided some cover. Hauck was betting that they did not realize how badly Otoktay had been hurt. The fire they had received in exchange for their own might have made them cautious. Chances were that they had melted away into the nearby canyon. In any event he had no choice.

He staggered on, breathless and blinded by snow, his back aching under its load, until he found himself among the rocks at the foot of the escarpment. Some of them were large and it was easy to find a place of concealment. As gently as he could he laid Otoktay down. The Indian's battered face was lined with pain and sweat was standing out on his forehead.

Quickly Hauck made a rough tourniquet out of his neckerchief and fastened it around Otoktay's leg above the wound in an attempt to stem the bleeding. He tore a strip of material and stuffed it inside the Indian's shirt against the bullet wound in his shoulder. It was the bullet which had ricocheted and it appeared to have made a clean wound. As far as Hauck could tell, nothing was broken.

'Looks like I might be getting my wish after all,' Otoktay said.

'Don't talk,' Hauck replied. 'Save your strength.'

Again the Indian grinned. 'It's OK,' he said. 'It had to come sometime and if I was to choose, it would be something like this.'

The first necessity was for warmth and Hauck set about making a fire using materials from Otoktay's pack. When he had it going he made coffee and laced it with whiskey from a flask. He held out a tin cup to Otoktay, who took it in both hands.

'We need to get you back down the mountain,' Hauck said.

'Don't worry about me. Just get Birds Landing.'

Hauck was thinking rapidly. How was he to get Otoktay back down the mountain? He could build some sort of travois but nothing grew at this altitude. Maybe the outlaws had brought up their horses, but he doubted it. Standing up, he looked out at the dense, driving snow. He should probably attempt to dig out the bullet in the Indian's leg, try to make some sort of splint. Otoktay had already lost a lot of blood. Behind him the fire was sputtering as snowflakes landed in it. He turned to Otoktay. The old Sioux warrior was lying back, his head propped against the rock, his shattered leg extended. His eyes were open. Hauck moved towards him.

'Otoktay,' he said.

There was no reply and Hauck realized that Otoktay was dead. He sank to his knees beside the fire, overwhelmed by a grief such as he had never known before. It was like a physical shock, but it did not last. In its place there came a cold, icy determination to seek retribution, to deal with the men who had killed his friend and still held captive his woman.

Sitting by Otoktay, he closed his eyes and held him in his arms. For the first time he realized that Otoktay had been struck not twice but three times. The third bullet had hit him in the back, narrowly missing the spine, but evidence of it had been concealed by the pack he carried. Although it was the least conspicuous of his wounds, it was probably the one that had killed him.

After a time Hauck got to his feet. The fire had gone out and he felt an urgent need to act. Carefully he laid his friend on the ground beside the rock. Snow fell on the Indian's upturned face and had already began to cover him. There was little Hauck could do. He began to look for rocks to pile on Otoktay's body, but there was really no point.

Leaving Ototkay to the wind and the weather and to the mountains on high, Hauck set off with grim determination to seek his killers. He knew they could not be far away. They were probably looking to kill him almost as much as he was looking to kill them. He walked along the bottom of the cliff, seeking the point at which he imagined they had been waiting in ambush. He found plenty of evidence in the form of spent shells.

There was something else, too. In places which the snow had not covered there were bloodstains. It seemed that at least one of the outlaws had been shot. Hauck moved to the cleft behind the rockfalls. The entrance to the canyon was steep and rocky. Hauck scrambled over the boulders and climbed up what would, in summer, have been a narrow watercourse. He was in the bed of a stream, and as he clambered higher it began to level out. He moved forward more quickly, working on the assumption that Dement and his men were ahead of him, his senses alert.

After moving a little further he saw something which surprised him: the fading imprint of horses' hoofs. They couldn't have come up the way he had done, so they must have entered from the other side. He was in a pass which led through the mountain and then probably down from the high ranges. Further along there were horse droppings. He was getting close to them now. What would they be doing?

He tried to put himself in their place. The ambush they had set had not achieved its aim. They might assume that they had shot at least one of their pursuers but they could not know how badly he was hurt. They had retreated into the canyon. He had seen nothing of them so it was fair to conclude that they were somewhere ahead of him, waiting to see if they were followed.

He didn't want to run straight into another bush-whacking. He looked about him. The canyon walls got steeper further along but at this point he could reach the top of the escarpment. Leaving his pack behind some rocks, he slung his rifle across his shoulder and started to climb.

At last he reached the top and staggered over the rim, to be met by a howling wind which almost knocked him over. When he turned to follow the contour of the canyon the wind was at his back. The snow was driven hard against him but when he looked up the sky seemed clearer. Dark clouds scudded across but it was not the blank uniform grey of the previous few days. There wasn't much daylight left.

Hauck paused to take in his surroundings. To his left was the edge of the cliff with the canyon winding down below. On the other side of the canyon the ridge continued, falling way into the distance. To his right stretched an empty high plateau and beyond that he could just make out the dim shapes of mountains. He resolved to follow the rim of the canyon. His hand hurt and his head wound was bleeding again. He began to walk, wishing he still had his snowshoes, but he had left them behind with the other things that weren't strictly necessary.

Every now and then he stopped to look over the rim for any sign of

Dement or his henchmen. He was almost certain they were up ahead and he was also confident that they would be waiting for him to come through the canyon. He hoped that they would not anticipate that he would get above them. It was unlikely he would be seen but his senses were alert to any indications of danger.

As darkness approached the wind dropped and the snow began to slacken. Night descended and patches of sky could be seen between the clouds. A few stars flickered but there was no moon. Conditions were in Hauck's favour. If he could locate the outlaws he would have the cover of darkness. It was bitterly cold now but Hauck barely felt it. All his attention was on finding Dement and his gunslicks. He couldn't be wrong. Surely they were somewhere ahead of him?

He continued walking, going slightly downhill now. Again he approached the edge of the plateau and looked over. It was very dark down there with lighter patches of drifted snow. He peered closely. He couldn't be sure but after a few moments of concentrated gaze he thought he saw a faint glow a long way ahead. It might not be anything, or it might be the reflection of a fire.

He stepped back from the edge and resumed walking till, looking down into the canyon again, he saw that the glow had grown more definite. He was certain that it was from the gunmen's campfire. He quickened his pace, the snow crunching and crackling beneath his tread, being careful to avoid any treacherous drifts. The ridge was lower at this point; it took a slight turn and then he saw the fire. A short distance away he thought he could make out a rough corral with horses in it.

Around the camp fire a number of men were seated. In the lurid firelight he counted five. One of them appeared to have his arm in a rough sling. They were drinking and smoking cigarettes. He looked hard for Birds Landing but he couldn't see her. He drew back from the cliff edge and moved further until he was directly above the camp. Then he crawled forward on his hands and knees. Yes, there were five of them.

Then, just beyond the range of the firelight and close to the further wall of the canyon he saw what at first sight seemed to be just another mound of snow or a rock. Peering more closely, he saw that it was some sort of bundle, some kind of covering that might conceal another person.

'Birds Landing!' he breathed.

There was no way he could be certain but it was a reasonable surmise. If so it was the first evidence he had that she was still alive. A huge emotion seized him compounded of a multiplicity of conflicting elements: joy, relief, anxiety. As was always the case when the situation demanded it was soon replaced by a cold, hard concentration at the core of him.

He assessed the situation. He could just open fire with his rifle, but it was too risky. The light was not good. It was unlikely that he would finish them all off. Birds Landing would be at risk in the crossfire, or she might be deliberately killed. Once they were aware of his presence they would have the advantage. Coming at them in this fashion had served its purpose. He needed to get closer, to be on the same level in order to defend Birds Landing.

He looked along the ridge. Further ahead it dipped; it should be possible to climb down. If he came on them from that direction he would have an extra edge because they wouldn't be expecting it. He crawled back until there was no possibility of being seen from below, then continued to move along the top of the cliff, going steadily downhill.

When he judged that he was a sufficient distance from the camp he approached the lip once more. He was well beyond the corral and the fire had shrunk to an insignificant flickering gleam.

He lowered himself over the edge and began to move on his haunches till he reached a steeper part. Then he slowly clambered over rocks and shale till he had almost reached the bottom. The last bit was difficult and there seemed to be no way he could reach the canyon floor other than by jumping. It was a good way down and he was concerned about making any sound. He hovered for a moment or two searching for any other way of descent. The wind carried the snicker of a horse to his ears.

Not being able to find any alternative, he focused his attention, drew a deep breath and sprang from the rock. He landed heavily, losing his rifle in the process, but the snow came to his rescue, cushioning his fall and deadening any noise he might otherwise have made. He fell forward and felt his leg jar, but he was all right.

He lay still for a few moments while he gathered himself together and waited for any movement coming from the direction of the camp before getting to his feet. Leaning against the canyon wall, he considered searching for the rifle, but it was dark and he didn't want either to delay or cause any noise. Instead he checked his Colts. He put one back in its holster, hefted the other in his hand and crept stealthily and silently towards the firelight, hugging the darkest parts of the path as he went.

He wasn't sure exactly what he intended to do, except reach the outlaw camp without being detected and then make contact with Birds Landing. Shielded as he was by the night the first part at least should not be too difficult. He was close enough now to pick up odd scraps of conversation and was approaching the corral when everything changed.

Picking up his scent, one of the horses began to snort. Hauck heard a voice coming out of the darkness.

'Whoa there, fella!'

He stopped in his tracks, pressing into the wall of the canyon. The horses were restless and he could hear them stamping. Another voice spoke but he could not catch the words. Further down the canyon he saw the figure of a man outlined against the fire, then another voice called.

'Everything OK back there?'

Emerging from the darkness behind the corral a figure appeared on the path only yards from where Hauck was standing against the rock.

'Something spooked the horses!' the man shouted back.

Hauck was still hoping the alert would blow over when suddenly the muffled sound of footsteps came from behind him and a shot smashed into the rock wall above his head. He had no choice. Stepping into the path he fired as a running figure bore down on him and another shot ricocheted near by. The man screamed and went crashing to the floor as Hauck turned and fired at the other man, who was standing in the path ahead of him. Almost simultaneously the man returned fire but it was dark and both shots missed.

For a moment they both stood

immobile, but in that brief time Hauck recognized the figure of Dement. It wasn't just the man's appearance: some instinct told him that it was the man he had come looking for.

Hauck began to run, zigzagging from side to side. As flame spurted from Dement's gun and another bullet went whining down the canyon he smashed into him with his shoulder, bowling him over and leaving him stunned. Hauck kept running. He had only one thing in mind, and that was to reach Birds Landing. He had both guns out now and was blazing away at the shadowy figures ahead of him. They had been taken by surprise and were slow to realize what was happening. Two of them went down and Hauck could see two others.

Stabs of flame illumined the night and the noise of gunfire was deafening as it reverberated around the canyon. The horses were charging about in the corral, rearing and neighing in their agitation, and from that direction another scream rose into the night air. Hauck heard a crash and then the sound of galloping hoofs. He didn't need to turn round to realize that some of the horses had broken loose and were stampeding in a panic along the path behind him.

Instinctively Hauck veered towards the tumbled rocks at the foot of the cliff and hurled himself behind a boulder as the horses went crashing through the camp. One of the outlaws, the one with the bandaged arm, was running but down he went beneath the trampling hoofs. The other one blazed away at where Hauck had taken refuge. Shards of granite flew up and a bullet ricocheted around the enclosed space before cutting through the shoulder of Hauck's thick sheepskin jacket. Raising himself above the level of the rock, Hauck loosed two shots and the man slammed backwards into the fire.

With dread at his heart Hauck ran forward, looking for Birds Landing, not knowing what he might find. He saw the dark outline of the bundle where she had been lying, but it was empty. He looked around desperately and called her by her Indian name.

'Ealaothek-kaunis!'

The only reply was a staccato voice behind him. 'Drop your guns!'

Hauck instantly weighed up the situation. He could turn and fire but his chances were poor.

'Do it now!'

Hauck flung the Colts to one side, but not too far.

'OK, turn round and make it real slow.'

Hauck turned. The man was holding a rifle and it was aimed right at his chest. Behind him Dement was approaching.

'Kill him!' Dement shouted.

Dement had a pistol in his hand and now he raised it. The man with the rifle was momentarily distracted and gave a quick glance to his side. It was enough. Hurling himself sideways to where he had thrown his guns, Hauck snatched one up and rolled away, firing as he did so. The shot was a good one and blood spurted from the man's chest. He raised the rifle but it had suddenly grown heavy in his hands and the shot he fired as he crumpled thudded harmlessly into the ground.

Dement began to shoot and bullets tore up the earth near where Hauck was lying. Pausing just a moment to take aim, Hauck squeezed the trigger of his gun. There was a click. He was out of ammunition. He looked for the other weapon, but he had lost it in the dark.

He looked up. Dement was almost upon him and there was nothing he could do to escape his upraised gun. There was an ugly leer across Dement's face as he pointed the weapon at Hauck's head. There was a crashing booming explosion like a peal of thunder, but it hadn't come from Dement's gun. Swaying for a moment, Dement crashed to the floor almost on top of his intended victim.

Hauck rubbed his eyes and got

unsteadily to his feet. Through all the darkness and the turmoil he saw a figure approaching. He was disoriented and couldn't make out who it was. He made to bend down in search of his Colt, then he straightened up with joy plucking at his heart. It was Birds Landing.

She ran towards him and he stumbled forward to meet her. The next moment she was in his arms. For what might have been an age they clung together before turning back to the scenes of mayhem behind them.

Hauck strode over to the inert form of Dement. He was dead, shot through the heart. Walking back towards the corral, Hauck found the bodies of the other gunmen and checked that they were dead also. Some of the horses had disappeared down the canyon; others were still restlessly moving about in the corral. Birds Landing came alongside him.

'What happened at the ranch?' she said. 'I was waiting at the mouth of the canyon when I heard something, a loud roaring noise. Then shortly afterwards the riders appeared.'

'Are you sure you're OK,' Hauck said, ignoring her words.

'I'm fine. They didn't have time to consider anything other than getting away. They knew you were behind them.'

She looked about as if expecting to see Rascombe, Hobbs and Otoktay. 'Where are the others?' she asked.

Quickly Hauck told the story of what had happened. When he got to the part about Otoktay he halted, fighting back the emotion which suddenly threatened to overcome him. Taking Birds Landing into his arms once more, he held her close, pressing his face into her hair.

'Otoktay is dead,' he managed to say at last. 'He died saving my life.'

They stood close together for a long time, than Hauck stepped back and, holding Birds Landing's face up, kissed her on her brow and on her eyelids.

'It's all right,' he said. 'Let me tell you about it.'

Together they returned to where the campfire blazed and Hauck finished his tale. Then they lay in each other's arms. Once this night was over, when the darkness was dispelled, with the coming of a new day they would go back to where the canyon met the wide-open lofty heights and carry out the proper death ceremonials for Otoktay. They would say farewell and have no regrets. They would sing the ancient chants to the Great Spirit and then they would leave together. They would make their way down a new trail while the old Indian remained for ever among the high, wild and lonesome ranges where he would have wanted to be, far above the transitory world of change.

★   ★   ★

It was early in the morning when Hauck and Birds Landing arrived at Scott Corner. The marshal was leaning against a post and looked up as they rode by. Two more drifters to keep an eye on, he thought. Then he looked more closely and his jaw fell open in surprise.

'Hauck!' he called. 'And Birds Landing! What in tarnation are you doin' here?'

Hauck looked across at the marshal. 'Harper!' he called.

He and Birds Landing slipped from their saddles. After tying their horses to the hitchrack they followed the marshal inside his office.

'Well,' Harper said. 'It's sure unexpected seein' you folks back in town. What you been doin' since I last saw you? Seems like a while ago.'

'It's a long story,' Hauck replied.

The marshal took a long look at them both. 'Hell,' he said, 'it's sure good to see you both.'

'How's Wendell Riley?' Hauck said.

'Wendell? He's fine now. Took him a time to get over what happened, but he's OK. Fact of the matter is he's got somethin' else on his mind right now.'

'Yeah? And what would that be?'

'Him and Hester. Goldurn it, he's finally roped her in and they're gettin' married next month.'

Birds Landing laughed and clapped her hands.

'Hey,' the marshal said. 'I reckon they'd be right glad to have you at the ceremony. Wendell still talks about you both. That is, if you plan on bein' around that long.'

Hauck turned to Birds Landing. There was a smile on both their faces.

'We'll be around,' Hauck said.

'That's good news. I guess you folks have plans but it'd be real nice to catch up on things.'

'There'll be plenty of time,' Birds Landing said. She turned to Hauck as if expecting him to add something.

'Fact is, Marshal,' he said, 'we're just not as young as we used to be. We been thinkin' the time has maybe come for us to start settlin' down. And Scott Corner seems as good a place as any.'

We do hope that you have enjoyed reading this large print book.

Did you know that all of our titles are available for purchase?

We publish a wide range of high quality large print books including:
**Romances, Mysteries, Classics
General Fiction
Non Fiction and Westerns**

Special interest titles available in large print are:
**The Little Oxford Dictionary
Music Book, Song Book
Hymn Book, Service Book**

Also available from us courtesy of Oxford University Press:
**Young Readers' Dictionary
(large print edition)
Young Readers' Thesaurus
(large print edition)**

For further information or a free brochure, please contact us at:
**Ulverscroft Large Print Books Ltd.,
The Green, Bradgate Road, Anstey,
Leicester, LE7 7FU, England.
Tel:** (00 44) **0116 236 4325
Fax:** (00 44) **0116 234 0205**

THE DEVIL'S PAYROLL

Paul Green

When bounty hunter John Harrison captures fugitive outlaw Clay Barton, he's persuaded by Maggie Sloane to allow the captive to lead them to the loot robbed from an army payroll. But Barton double-crosses them and the mysterious Leo Gabriel kidnaps Maggie. With a veteran Buffalo Soldier, Sergeant Eli Johnson, at his side, Harrison battles ruthless vaqueros and a Comanche war party to recover the money, re-capture Barton and rescue Maggie . . . but a surprise awaits him when he finally catches up with his enemies . . .

HELL ON HOOFS

Lance Howard

Arriving in Lancerville, John Laramie hoped to escape his old life as a man-hunter and settle down. But there he finds he's torn between the demons of his past and hope for a brighter future when a young woman seeks his help in getting rid of a vicious outlaw. Then the Cross Gang attacks him and the young woman's life is put in danger. But will it cost Laramie more to win than to lose in a deadly showdown?

TROUBLE AT MESQUITE FLATS

Will Keen

Arriving in Mesquite Flats, ex-New York businessman Bodene Rich is committed to Yuma Penitentiary for a vicious assault. He's released, in light of new evidence, and pardoned by Warden Bradley Shaw. On the day of Rich's release, Shaw resigns, but an unknown gunman then shoots him dead on the trail. Rich once again is in trouble. And, in a showdown, he's embroiled in a bloody gun battle, where the outcome hangs in the balance until the final shot . . .

HELL STAGE TO LONE PINE

Jack Dakota

At Lone Pine Ranch, young Ben Brewer wants to prove himself to the owner, Morgan Hethridge and his beautiful daughter Josie. But Hethridge's rival is scheming to take over Lone Pine ranch. To protect the land, Brewer faces the feared gunhawk Calvin Choate. A desperate situation, until old timer Whipcrack Riley steps in. Will his wily ways and his skills driving a stagecoach be enough to help Brewer once the situation gets really rough and the bullets are flying?